Introduction - Obituary	3-9
1.	William Lacey's England	10-24
2.	William's Sixteenth Birthday, 1851	25-35
3.	the Crimean War 1855	36-64
4.	Off to the Crimea	65-74
5.	Home	75-79
6.	Indian	80-98
7.	India	99-121
8.	Amelia	122-137
9.	Marriage	138-146
10.	Back to England	147-149
11.	England 1870	150-162
12.	Postscript	163-163
13.	Correspondence	164

INTRODUCTION

In 1919, the *Mansfield Gazette* reported:

Crimean Veteran's death (1835-1919)[1] – with military honours. The funeral took place at Mansfield Cemetery on Tuesday of a veteran of the Crimean war and Indian Mutiny, ex-sergeant William Lacey. The old gentleman, who died at Mexborough on Friday last, served for many years in the cavalry, enlisting in 1855 in the Royal Irish dragoon Guards (motto "who shall separate us?"), a regiment which was annihilated almost to a man in the famous charge of the Light Brigade at Balaclava.

He was trained with the 7th Hussars (nickname 'the Saucy 7th), motto, "honi soit qui mal y pense" in York and drafted out to the Crimea at the end of the same year but arrived too late to take part in any of the fighting of that memorable campaign, for the Armistice was completed just as the troopship reached harbour. After a flying visit to Sebastopol, his regiment was ordered to winter quarters in Scutari and returned home to England when peace was proclaimed.

In 1857, at the time of the Indian Mutiny, Mr Lacey volunteered to go with the 2nd Dragoon Guards to India and was quartered at Cawnpore until after the

---

[1] Quoted from the *Mansfield Gazette*.

fall of Lucknow, taking part in a couple of skirmishes with the enemy towards the close of the fighting. In 1862, by which time he had reached sergeant's rank, he left his regiment in Benares to take up staff employment, which he held until 1870, when he was invalided out of the service.

Sergeant Lacey married a native girl (5th January, 1864), who bore him eleven children (actually fourteen – three were left in India when they returned to England in 1870.[2]) They couple celebrated their Golden wedding in Mansfield in 1914, and Mrs Lacey died four years later.

The old gentleman, who was over 80 years of age was well known and respected in the town and, in addition to numerous members of the family who were present at the cemetery, the last rites were witnessed by a large number of people. A firing squad from a local company of the Sherwood Foresters preceded the cortege to the cemetery with arms reversed and at the conclusion of the service fired a volley over the grave. He lived at Stockwell Gate, Mansfield.

***

William's daughter (the author's grandmother, Rose Merry) had never mentioned her Indian mother and soldier father and for the rest of my life I regretted I

---

[2] *either because the children were too young to travel, or because the couple had too much on their hands*

was too young to question her about her past. Her son, my own father, was equally silent: in fact, I was one eighth Indian, but the family had "buried" my history for reasons best known to themselves - perhaps, in the British post-colonial racist climate that viewed Indians as "niggers", they were trying to protect me from some imaginary shame.

The following story is a reconstruction of my Great grandfather, William and Amelia Lacey's life, combining what I know with what I have had to "invent" from my knowledge of history - history plus fiction – or what you might call "faction" (with its inevitable friction).

This, of course, is what historians do all the time in their "interpretations" because facts do not speak for themselves: for example, my Census records[3] have Christopher and William Laceys going back to 1670 (with the exception of one named Job!), but, confusingly, give William's birth variously, as *about 1837*, or *1837/39*; and his father's, *about 1799*. So that even facts can often be interpreted – especially when one is looking for human motives, which brings us into the realm of fiction and guesswork.

The difficulties of turning fragmented family hearsay into historical truth were spelled out in Professor Ian Talbot's [4] reply to my suggestion that I do a PhD in

---

[3] Since 1801

[4] Southampton University History Department

order to discover more about William's life with the help of the professor's expertise:

Dear Sam,

Many thanks for your enquiry and try-out preface to your great grandfather William's story. As you are aware, the writing and researching tasks involved in a doctoral dissertation and in the kind of book you may intend (I had mentioned the possibilities for an 'exciting story') are not one and the same thing, though this does not mean they are irreconcilable. The case study (for this is what it would be) in a doctoral setting would require justification, setting in the existing literature and a clear methodological framework. Moreover, there is the issue of whether a single case study could be used to interrogate existing understandings. Finally, the issue of sources would need to be carefully considered.

All this to one side, I was fascinated by your preface. It raised a number of questions which you may be able to address. Begum (my family's word to describe great grandmother) was the title given for Muslim rather than Hindu ladies. Benares, or Varanasi (her home), was, however, a Hindu rather than Muslim-dominated city. Her name (Amelia Padham) is certainly not Muslim, nor is it Hindu), unless it is an Anglicised version of a Hindi name. It has much more the ring of a Eurasian name, although I may be wrong here.

The whole story of William Lacey visiting a rich Indian home in Benares is odd, given both your grandfather's rank (sergeant), the date cited and Roberts' involvement. British military officials did not make a practice of socialising with Indians in their own homes post-1857. If they had occasion to meet, it would be in more official settings, unless the individual concerned was of princely rank and had invited them on a hunting expedition. British commanding officers might be accompanied by ADC's, but these invariably did not rise through the ranks, or have non-commissioned status.

Post 1857, British Other Ranks were discouraged from relationships with Indians, let alone marrying them and staying in the service. BOR's, as they were called, might marry Anglo-Indians (Eurasians) and bring them back to England.

The family story is thus fascinating as it does not fit the common understanding of post-Mutiny mores. This does not mean it is untrue, but it would require careful corroboration. It should be possible to track a wedding certificate produced in Benares (possibly available in the BL) which might answer the identity question. If a wealthy Indian married a BOR it would be shockingly newsworthy and should also have a report in the press. It may even be possible to check the wealthy Hindu families in Benares, as the British kept such records and published them as a means of social control.

So, there are more questions than answers at present. All known factors at the time would certainly point to marrying Eurasian, but the barriers of marriage with a Hindu or Muslim lady, if they were of rank, would be almost insuperable. The army would have frowned on marriage with "a lower rank of Indian". Indeed, it would have formed a basis for dismissal from service in the post 1857 atmosphere. Yet your great grandfather served for a number of years afterwards.

It might be better to get to the bottom of these intriguing questions, first.

***

And so, with a large dose of assured ignorance, I begin the story of my great grandfather and his wife, hopefully filling gaps with intelligent historical guesswork, hoping that my lack of knowledge will not "hobble the story with dramatic inertia".[5]

I must therefore confess to complicating this novel by interpolating my own historical character [6] in order to explore through my great grandparents historical themes and questions in England that have long fascinated me: among them factory work, poverty, British imperialism (including racism), Victorian religion and the treatment of women.

---

[5] As one critique described the 2018 Mike Leigh film, *Peterloo*
[6] I am a historian

In this I have taken the liberty of attributing to my great grandparents perhaps more intellectual curiosity than they might have had, for pondering their experiences has had on me the liberating effect of empathy, tearing the veil of distance to bring me closer to their times.

WILLIAM LACEY'S VICTORIAN ENGLAND

The year was 1851, the first in England that more people lived for the first time in towns and cities, rather than the countryside. The Lacey's had just moved from Burton-On-Trent, Staffordshire, to Mansfield, Notts, shortly before Queen Victoria came to the throne in 1837 and their new home at 19, Pleasley Hill, Mansfield, was near the Cotton Mills that would provide employment for the whole family, except father Christopher, who was still a groom at Pleasley vicarage – a connection with the older, rural England and a reminder of the great changes now taking place in England.

Elizabeth (nine) was the youngest sister, followed by Caroline (fifteen), William (sixteen), Jane (eighteen), Mary (twenty-five) and the eldest, Christopher (thirty). Unlike his siblings William, was less than happy at Pleasley mill: he dreamed of adventure and was planning to do something about it.

His father was born in the Mansfield countryside in 1800 and few cities were pleasant places to live, even though they were the cause of the new wealth, for they often representing the worst in the nation's degeneracy, despite Britain's industrial superiority. De Tocqueville saw nearby Manchester's noisy, towering factories, teeming with energy, as "a foul drain" and "a filthy sewer"; and despite the fact that from it flowed "pure gold", it was "most brutish" and its men were "savages".

Poverty and dirt were its main cause, for the growing capitalist wealth besmirched the old English landscape with soot, overcrowding and pollution, causing enormous misery in industrial parts and in horrible London, with dirty, cramped living conditions, high rents, poisonous water supplies, disease, dirt, putrefaction and broken windows; when all workers had was their wage, which Florence Nightingale noted paid "worse than thieving".

Governments did not see it as part of their business to house workers, who had to live close to their employment in order to walk there and could be turned out at the drop of a hat if landlords did not like them. The empire was more important than Britain's working men and socialism was a foreign evil, reminding capitalists of disorderly 18th century France. The poor were kept in order either by compulsion or by their suffering. Very few politicians worried about social disruption, though Trades Unions were on the rise.

Pleasley Vale had the advantage of being rural and immune from these big city effects, so that fields round it were pure, leading in the distance to the village of Shirebrook, even if inside its factories shared the same human defects as those in the big cities.

In his 1834 Poor Law, Prime Minister Melbourne had revealed what politicians thought of ordinary workers the year before William's birth, in forcing the destitute into inhuman workhouses, whereas before, local rates had fed people in their own homes. And when queen Victoria asked he Prime Minister if he would read Dickens' *Oliver Twist*, he said it would be too "boring... all among workhouses, coffin makers and pickpockets. I don't like them in reality, therefore I don't wish to see them represented."

Dicken's *Pickwick Papers* had described an older, "Merry" England in the year of William's birth, but things were changing fast: capitalism was now king and universal free trade the new battle cry, after Prime Minister Peel. The poor were exploited, manipulated and ignored, despite producing Britain's vast new wealth.

The new Age of Steam had established the powerfully-irresistible mechanical principle, allowing Britain to lead the world and generate great wealth by buying raw materials abroad and re-exporting them as factory produce. It was for many an exciting time to be alive: nearly a half of world trade now passed through British ports, which produced forty percent of all manufactured goods and two thirds of textiles in its world monopoly.

But, despite a world-wide empire, banking system, and all-powerful fleet, most of the world's merchant ships and the transplantation of British across the globe - awful working conditions were improving only slowly in Pleasley Vale's noisy, polluting cotton factories. As steam ships now allowed increased travel and "Railway Mania" was rapidly shrinking

England with reduced ticket prices for workers, allowing them to see their own country for the first time, William was dreaming of a new life.

He knew the 19th century was Britain's moment in world history and he wanted to be part of this marvellous new world, spinning "forever down the ringing groves of change". He was excited to hear about grand new railway stations and bridges, with amazing train speeds of 30mph and, like many boys since, dreamed of becoming an engine driver. It was as if Nature had been conquered and time abolished: amazingly, only ten years after William was born, he could get from London to Birmingham in five-and-a-half hours; and in his teens, London to York. He dreamed of travel - he did not yet know where - but he was determined, "by hook or by crook", as father Christopher would say.

Where this determination came from was difficult to determine, but two generations later in the middle of the twentieth century, two of his subsequent family also went abroad, marrying in Singapore and China, an indication, perhaps that his restless desire to travel would be inherited down to the third generation, though in their case not to fight a war, but to teach.

The Industrial Revolution's unprecedented transformation in iron, steel, machines and financial capitalism meant people no longer starved through limitations of muscle power in agriculture, as they had in 1840's Ireland, forcing millions to escape to England, Canada and Australia.

At his desk in the British Library, Marx was at that time brilliantly describing what he called "the commodification of life" at work in a new slavery - capitalist exploitation. So much, thought William, for the joys of work - with its long hours, desperate poverty, bad housing and terrible sanitation, which had brought from India - amongst other diseases – the dreaded cholera in the 1830's, which William would later see at first hand in India, from which it came.

"Father, do you think things are really improving for us factory workers?" asked William after a day at his factory.

"Well, compared with the Peterloo Massacre of 1819, when I was eighteen, you might say that there has been some improvement – but not much."

"What happened at Peterloo, father?"

"A huge crowd of peaceful, ordinary people - sixty thousand - came to Manchester one Monday morning with banners demanding "Liberty and Fraternity", against unjust "Taxation without Representation" – they had no vote. Bands played *Rule Britannia* and *God Save the King* and it all began cheerfully enough - among the northern contingents were two hundred women from Oldham, dressed in white, with children and picnics."

"What, did they really want, father?"

"Parliamentary reform, son. Getting the vote would force rich politicians to listen to us ordinary folk. But troops were sent in: eighteen dead, six-hundred-and-fifty injured – one of the bloodiest political clashes in our history. We were up against selfish land and factory-owning superiors who refused to share power. They will do anything to stop us workers organizing to gain political equality."

Father went to his cupboard and took out an old copy of *the Times*: "unlike *the Manchester Mercury*, which blamed the people, the *Times* told the truth," he said and began reading an article by its reporter, John Tyas:

The Yeoman Cavalry were seen advancing in a rapid trot – their ranks in disorder – and stopped to breathe their horses and recover their ranks. A panic seemed to strike the people at the outskirts of the meeting, who immediately began to scamper in every direction.

After a moment's pause, the cavalry drew their swords and brandished them fiercely in the air, upon which Hunt desired the multitude to give three cheers to show the military the people were not daunted by their unwelcome presence (and would stand firm).

He had scarcely said these words before the Manchester yeomanry rode into the mob, which gave way before them. Then the whole troop wheeled round and surrounded the people in such a manner to prevent their escape...cutting indiscriminately to right and left...setting the people running in all directions. Then, brick bats were thrown by the crowd and the Manchester Yeomanry lost all command of temper.

A man within five yards of us had his nose completely taken off by a sabre blow, whilst another was laid prostrate, but whether he was dead or had merely thrown himself down to obtain protection, we cannot say. Feeling great alarm, we saw a constable at no great distance and thinking that our only chance of safety lay in placing ourselves under his protection, we appealed to him. He immediately took us into custody and when we told him we were writers, he replied, "Oh! Oh! you are one of their writers – you must go before the magistrates".

On our road thither, we saw a woman on the ground insensible, with two large gouts of blood on her left breast. The constables were treating Hunt in a manner they were neither justified by law or humanity, striking him with their staves on his head.

William now folded the paper and replaced it in his cupboard like a valuable treasure.

He then began to read the words of Samuel Bamforth, a weaver who had witnessed the killing and wanted universal suffrage:

Several mounds of human beings still remained where they had fallen, crushed down and smothered – some of these were still groaning, while others, with staring eyes, were gasping for breath, and others would never breathe more. Persons might sometime be noticed peeping from attics and over the tall ridging of houses, but they quickly withdrew, as if fearful of being observed, or unable to sustain the full gaze of a scene so hideous and abhorrent.

"60,000 peaceful demonstrators, fifteen deaths and six hundred injuries. This was the beginning of reform in England, so resented by our masters."

"Monday morning was a strange time to hold a political rally, wasn't it, Father?"

"Ah, but handloom weavers working from home usually took Mondays off after working all weekend. They wanted representation and a stop to rotten boroughs, like Old Sarum, which sent two MPs to Westminster with no votes."

"What's a rotten borough, father?"

"Places with no population that can elect MP's, where the landowner controls both the candidate and the vote – rotten British political corruption at its worst! Just like the Peterloo magistrates signing up four hundred special constables armed with long wooden truncheons, three-hundred-and-forty regular cavalry from the 15th Hussars and four hundred infantry armed with two six-pounder artillery cannon. In all, one-thousand-five-hundred soldiers and constables to stop a peaceful demonstration!

(Ironically, the 15th Hussars would be William's regiment when he later joined the army for the Crimea, though it was the inexperienced Manchester Yeomanry who caused the mayhem).

"There was a warrant for the arrest of the Peterloo organisers and mounted Yeomanry soon approached the crowd at speed. They knocked over a twenty-three-year-old woman and her baby son in the process, who fell under their hooves as first fatality of the day. People shouted "Soldiers! Soldiers!" and tried to escape."

"But father, they were doing nothing wrong, were they? England is the land of the free!"

"Don't kid yourself, son. Infantry blocked the streets near the field, so some took refuge in the yard surrounding the Quaker chapel. Others were crushed against walls, or fell down cellar steps surrounding buildings. The wounded tried to crawl away and in only twenty minutes, the field was cleared. The wounded – including children – tried to hide their injuries for fear of revenge from our masters and one man was driven into a lime pit and burned. And James Lees, a weaver who had fought at Waterloo, complained: 'At Waterloo there was man to man, but here it was downright murder.'

"Shelley wrote a poem – *the Masque of Anarchy*:

I met murder on the way

He had a mask like Castlereagh –

Very smooth he looked, yet grim;

Seven bloodhounds followed him

All were fat; and well they might

Be in admirable plight,

For one by one and two by two,

He tossed them human hearts to chew

Which from his wide cloak he drew."

"But what about the 1832 Reform Act, father? "

"Son, the Whigs only gave the vote to propertied middle classes, who were afraid of revolution, especially with a new Napoleon III in France. Parliament is at this moment discussing a Militia Bill for policing the likes of us - the Duke of Wellington always warned that any reform would be the beginning of revolution -

"But it's still a great time to be sixteen, William. England's changing fast and my old childhood communities are disappearing: more than half of us English now live in new towns and cities. Sure, life is a dirty complicated struggle to survive and there is a lot of hardship, but wages are gradually rising and your mother and all my children work at the mill, thank the Lord. So though we are not poor, many are."

"Some say the population is growing too fast, and there are too many people to feed, father."

"Malthus was right: growing population causes struggle - but standards **are** improving. And Chartism and the Anti-Corn Law League do not want revolution, only reform because the English are law-abiding and do not like disorder. You are all working and we are earning a decent wage."

"But I never see fresh air, father, and factory hours are very long, with no excitement - it's very dull. No wonder black is the main colour of clothes - it hides coal and smoke stains. The machine is now king, not farming seasons like when you were a boy - we are factory slaves, though I suppose you are right - it is better than starving, and wages are increasing slowly."

"Don't over-romanticise life in the countryside, son, even though it seemed more natural. Wages are definitely higher now, though yes, there is disease in the new towns, caused by bad drinking water - open sewers with no proper pipes and too much rubbish. We need earthenware, not leaking wooden pipes. And good water sources. Anyway, the new General Board of Health should allow local authorities to get sanitary powers if middle class rate payers are willing to pay, though I doubt it because they only want to save their money on the rates."

"Some people would rather catch cholera than have government telling them what to do," said William."

"Maybe, son, but there's too much typhoid and malnutrition – "

"And bronchitis because of bad ventilation in our factories. The Workhouse kids in my factory get ill because they are so malnourished."

"There is still much to be done, but mark my words, things will get better, son."

****

When William was ten, he had become a spinner in one of three cotton factories in the Vale in the new capitalist mills at Pleasley. He was now a wage labourer, along with his sisters.

In 1845, When he was twenty, two great open fields to the north of Mansfield, along with meadows to the south were fenced in, releasing building land. Evicted tenants now had to buy food they could no longer produce themselves because they were alienated from their former allotments. The inner city now spawned terrible slums and the 1834 Poor Law Amendment Act was a typically-cruel Victorian attempt to save money and label the poor undeserving criminals who had brought their fate on themselves. Anyone with nowhere to live had to go to a police station to get a ticket for a bed.

The Establishment clergy had generally agreed that the workhouse should be a place of hardship, coarse fare, degradation and humility – strict and severe, as repulsive as was consistent with humanity and conditions were deliberately bad to ensure people had to be really desperate to seek refuge: families were separated, men from women, children from mothers, with barely enough to eat, becoming in effect, slaves. They were stripped of their clothes, which were sterilized, and belongings were put in storage. Then they were washed, de-loused and disinfected with carbolic soap, before donning the uncomfortable workhouse uniform.

And, in an act reminiscent of future Nazi treatment of Jews, single women had to wear the yellow stripe of shame; while boys and men made fertilizer by grinding bones on which they often gnawed - or ate candles and potato peel.

William's father had told him that before he was born, three small boys aged between four and five, had been transferred to Fareham Workhouse in Hampshire, where they were harshly treated. They had previously got over problems of bed wetting, but the move upset them and they began again soiling their beds, Punishments failed to stop them, and increased in severity.

When the story appeared in *the Times*, a committee of investigation was set up: it was learned the boys had been made to wear dunces' caps, standing on a stool in a corner and hit with birch rods. When this did not work, stocks were introduced. Another punishment – only half of their usual amount of food for two or three days a week over a month, had no effect on their behaviour, but the boys became weak and ill. None of this had been agreed by the Workhouse Guardians.

At the end of January 1837, when William was two years old, these children were isolated in an outhouse, with a cold stone floor and no fireplace, only a hot air stove to warm the space.

Back in Bishops Waltham, a doctor nursed the boys back to health, but Jonathan Cooke needed special care and nearly died. The staff at Fareham Workhouse were found guilty of negligence.

***

Mansfield's Pleasley Vale was a pretty, deep, narrow valley formed where the River Meden had cut through limestone. By 1767, two forges and a corn mill were operating and in 1782, Pleasley Park was leased to construct three water-powered cotton mills for the East Midlands hosiery industry, where steam was introduced in the decade of William's birth.

William loved his sisters, but he sometimes felt silly telling people he worked in the cotton mill and dreamed of doing something more "manly", even though his spinning machine required strength and muscle. The crash and whirr of machines in his muggy factory was a constant problem, along with cotton dust clogging his dry throat and threatening illness. He yearned for fresh air.

True, there had been factory reforms and new Inspectors had brought in the Ten Hours Bill in 1847. But though his cotton mill was now supposed to be properly ventilated and clean, authority always favoured the whims of capitalist bosses, who could ignore the new rules. And hours were still long and hard, even though children under nine could no longer be employed and under-eighteen's not work before 5.30 am, or after 8. 30 p.m. William dreamed of escaping his prison mill. He pitied Workhouse apprentices, who were treated like the African slaves who had made Glasgow, Liverpool and Bristol shamefully rich.

The reasons for capitalist owners' opposition to factory reform were revealing: they said it interfered with "freedom" of labor and parental "rights" to let children work. Profit, not humanity, was their king and they complained that British industry would become uncompetitive on world markets; that reform would create a "dangerous" precedent for other trades.

They brazenly insisted mill owners could reform factories themselves and that restricting working hours was especially unfair to twenty-four-hour-a-day water-powered mills, like Pleasley. That machines were more important than human life and reform would make children unemployable.

They argued that fathers should be free to dispose of children's labour as they thought fit and with a family to feed, Christopher Lacey agreed. His wife and children supplemented his lean wage and, in any case, at the age of fifty-four, he was no longer as fit as he was at a time when most people were dead by forty.

Christopher had been assured that dangerous machinery was now securely fenced off and that no young person was allowed to clean it when in motion. In any case, his children were keen to go out and earn – not like the local young ragamuffins outside, running about unaccompanied when their parents worked.

Up to 400,000 of the county's cotton workers were left unemployed when the American Civil war stopped cotton from reaching England's north-west in the 1860s and the mills were closed. They supported the South – never mind slavery - because they needed the cotton and without work, they struggled to put food on the table during the cotton famine.

William's Sixteenth Birthday, 1851

On William's sixteenth birthday he came home early through streets smelling of horse dung and straw to a candle-dark house, taking care to wash himself down at the cold-water tap just outside and change from his work clothes. Later, sitting with father, candles lit, he reminisced about his short life and dreamed of a more exciting future.

Father entered, went to his cupboard and took out a book by a new author, Charles Dickens, published in the year of William's birth (1835). Then, with a humorous gleam in his eye, he read the first sentence:

"Your birth was like the first ray of light which illumed the gloom and converted to dazzling brilliance my life."

William laughed at this *Pickwick* quote and said, "You are joking – I was just another mouth to feed, along with brother Christopher and my sisters!"

"My children are the gold who keep us out of poverty - God bless you!" said Christopher, patting William on the head, before returning the book. He continued,

"Thank goodness things are slowly improving since Dickens wrote *Oliver Twist*. In the Hungry Forties, there was terrible Irish famine."

Father crossed himself before resuming:

"But, William, this exciting new world is also a very selfish one. Capitalism is destroying the old world of my youth. When I was a boy, each knew his place and everyone in the rural community supported each other. My mother and father worked at home, spinning, weaving and growing food on our little piece of land. But things are now changing, with modern machinery, railways, factories – I am very lucky still to be working with horses."

"I also love horses, father, thanks to you." Then, rather presciently, in view of how his life in the cavalry would turn out, William added, "There will always be a job for me with horses."

"We were healthy," continued father, "lots of fresh air and little contact with the town, until machinery robbed my father of his domestic trade. The squire was our natural superior, with help and advice, or settling our village disputes. There were few temptations to drink, as there now are in the factories. Children were near home all day, living lives near open fields and not abandoned by parents in the mills. They also feared God.

"We could not read or write - but we were happy. Now, the Industrial Revolution has made us all like our manufacturers' machines. Hargreaves' *Spinning Jenny* and the *Mule* destroyed my father's livelihood and mass production caused prices to fall so rapidly, we were forced to leave our land, which was taken over by large tenants buying us out."

"So you do not really think things are better now, Father?"

"Poverty is growing everywhere with new city slums and people looking for work in towns are losing the old ways – especially the Irish, after that terrible famine in your teens. Thank God we are a cut above these poor un-educated devils, living with their animals and drinking themselves to death. Fortunately, our family works in one of the new Pleasley factories, so I do not think we will starve."

Father crossed himself.

"And now there is a growing empire – **Great** Britain indeed! Our precious world trade has brought cholera from India and sometimes I think it is God's punishment for selfishness. Never go into trade, my son."

Mother Hannah now chipped in, "We moved from Burton-on-Trent to find jobs in new factories, powered by steam. They are noisy and suffocating. It is difficult to hear oneself speak and they are bad for the lungs - not to mention the heat and girls getting their hair tangled, fingers nipped off, and sucked into the machines."

"Steam makes everything quicker," said Father, "but the machine is now boss and we are **not** machines, despite what our bosses say."

"It was a shock when I started at the age of nine," continued Mother, "but at least we had a living. And there are worse jobs – "

"Aye," said Father, "like stone breaker."

"Or chimney sweep!" added William, laughing. "Since 1840, it has been illegal for anyone under the age of 21 to sweep chimneys, though I know several boys who still do it."

"Factory standards are terrible, with homes are all squashed together around them," said Mother.

"At least we don't live in Manchester or Liverpool," said William.

"But," said Father, "I miss my own village and the countryside - Pleasley Vale is no substitute. Still, no workhouse for us - yet!" he joked, "and factory conditions are slowly improving. Robert Peel stopped the employment of children under nine and gave you kids a twelve-hour day up to the age of sixteen."

"So, for the last seven years, children have only worked six-and-a-half hours and women 60 hours a week," said Mother.

"But not men!" added Father quickly, "and the inspectors often do nothing to enforce the law. Bad ventilation and increasing speed of machinery is very unhealthy. We now own nothing, except our labour, unlike when we lived in the countryside. Karl Marx is right about that – 'workers of the world unite, you have nothing to lose but the chains of your labour.' "

"You should see where some people have to live," said William, "whole families in one room. And disease! If it's not typhoid, it's tuberculosis, starvation and bad housing. There was another cholera outbreak only this year, wasn't there, father? It's killed thousands. I think it is bad water"

"If you join the army and go abroad, you are more likely to die of cholera than get killed in battle, son."

William wondered whether Father was beginning to get an inkling of his possible future plans.

"We need trades unions – and the vote," asserted Mother

"But not, I hope, this new Marxist revolution," responded Father. "The government is frightened because of the way mill owners treat us factory workers and understandably fear a Communist uprising".

"Three years ago, William, when you were thirteen, the French King was deposed. A *Communist Manifesto* was published and huge London demonstrations were planned by the Chartists. Our government feared the overthrow of the state and sent our Royals for safety to Osborne House on the Isle of Wight, while our police took up positions near important buildings in London.

"20,000 protesters gathered at Kennington Common and Chartist leaders took three cabs to Westminster to present a huge petition: but it was ignored and the revolution did not happen."

"So instead," interrupted Mother, "the government is now considering a Militia Bill in case of trouble 'at t' mill'."

William thought being in the Militia far more interesting than working in a mill with his sisters, though he did not want to do down his own working class brothers.

"Our aristocrat rulers don't want to give us the vote because they think we are unfit to make political judgements – the truth is we might change things to our advantage, not theirs."

"Yes," said mother, "and Peel's 'bobbies' were only created to stop Chartist marches. England's aristocratic politicians do not believe in democracy and never will, mark my words."

"No wonder people cheered when the Houses of Parliament burned down, father."

"Quite! We are in the middle of an economic experiment that has never been tried before. Karl Marx calls our society's central object the "commodity" – getting and spending - which makes nonsense of other values. Life is hard and raw in this new capitalist economy of wealth plus absolute poverty. Life seems nothing but hardship in the black atmosphere of chimneys and flaming furnaces. The price of the new factory discipline is hard work – or the workhouse! In England we even have to work on Sunday, such is the joy of working!

"But, son, let us remember that it is also an exciting time: this century is Britain's moment in world history. We are the most successful state ever, even more than the Romans, though not perhaps the happiest. Our working class has not revolted like the French: the Chartist movement has collapsed and the 1832 Reform Act has stopped revolution, thank God!"

Father appeared very comforted by this observation.

"Our first railway station at Euston allows capitalists to move their stuff round quicker in England and send it off from our ports in new steamers to the rest of the world, but I do not think the Industrial Revolution will make us happier: it is creating mill slaves with no hope of betterment - a world of haves and have-nots."

"You mean like us, father."

"As Marx said, wage earners have nothing without work because they own no property. Just before you were born, the Tolpuddle Martyrs got seven year's transportation simply for forming a union, swearing an oath and complaining they had to live on nine shillings a week.

"One of the Tolpuddle Martyrs, wrote

*God is our guide! from field, from wave,
From plough, from anvil, and from loom;
We come, our country's rights to save,
And speak a tyrant faction's doom:
We raise the watch-word liberty;
We will, we will, we will be free!*

"But there are now laws against poaching, so that the rich can massacre game for pleasure."

In bed that night with an aching body and sounds from his nearby mill, William thought about father's words. His own mill job in pretty Meden Vale with Hannah, his mother and sisters was tolerable, but spinning was boring and he wanted to discover what life was really all about. The mill's noisy machines drowned out the Meden river and he woke every morning with their noise in his head. His sisters never complained, but surely there must be a better life?

He would rather work with Dad at the vicarage – at least he would be outside with horses, like in the old days before factories. Life now seemed worse, despite railways, canals and steam ships. Peel's Corn Laws had allowed cheaper food, but this just meant factory owners could pay lower wages and free trade meant more wealth for capitalists.

Fire had destroyed the old Parliament building, but the medieval social system was still in place, of which the new building was a feudal copy. Medieval elites were still in control of government. Individuals were not free and there were two nations – rich and poor.

At sixteen, the 1851 Great Exhibition showed that Britain dominated 41% of the world's trade and William wanted to be part of this exciting "workshop of the world": but how? What could he do in this new Empire on which the sun never set?

Britain was now the world's banker and London the centre of finance (which was not part of William's expertise); and though Liverpool linked the cotton of the American south with Lancashire factories, he had had enough of cotton factories, for the moment. But there were other considerations: tea from China, wool from Australia, sugar from the Caribbean.

He knew England was not healthy - even small towns like his Mansfield were poisoned by human, animal and industrial waste. Coal mines may provide domestic warmth, but they were beginning to pollute and darken the skies, causing respiratory disease and foul drinking water, which in turn encouraged Cholera and Typhoid.

Crystal Palace was at that time displaying British world success in the greatest city in the world; but, as *Punch* pointed out, the greatest service the Exhibition could do for England was a to produce a glass of water that was fit to drink in "stinking London, with its rancid Thames".

William knew only about spinning and looking after father's horses at Pleasley vicarage. Mansfield was building houses with lack of sanitation and poor drains – and even Prince Albert's Windsor Castle was bad enough to kill Prince Albert with Typhoid by 1861.

That night, on his sixteenth birthday, as William thought about life chances in his cotton Mill and a life expectation of only twenty-six in Liverpool, he finally decided to do something to change his life. It might slip away unless he did something to change it for the better, even though things were supposedly starting to improve. There was something wrong: how could he belong to a nation that ruled the world through its great empire and yet live so impoverished a life.

Thanks to Gladstone's 1844 Railway Act "the parliamentary train" was put on every route, allowing people to travel at a minimum speed of twelve miles an hour. But William also wanted to see something of the British Empire and his thoughts turned to joining the army.

Britain was now the greatest imperial power in Canada, South Africa, Australia, India and the West Indies. From India, it had already expanded into Burma, the Sind and the Punjab, now more important than Hong Kong and Shanghai. Twenty-two million people had migrated since 1815 and it was difficult to choose where to go. But History was about to decide for him in the shape of the Crimean War.

The Crimean War 1853-6

One summer's day in 1853 when William was eighteen, he picked up father's newspaper and read: "Russia invades the Danube principalities of Wallachia and Moldavia and refuses to leave". Britain announced it was sending a fleet to the Dardanelles, to be joined by France.

"What does it all mean, father?"

"The Russians are threatening the Turkish Empire, son, and therefore Europe."

"What has it got to do with us in England?"

"Well, it may mean they have their eyes on Afghanistan and our India. And there is also tension over the Holy Places in Palestine, controlled by Turkey: the Russian Orthodox Church want them and so does the new Emperor, Napoleon III of France."

"We surely don't want another war with France, Father."

"No, son, the new Napoleon is very friendly. He came here after laughable failures at revolution in France, the year after you were born. We have nothing to fear from him: though he is trying to imitate his famous uncle, he is really only 'a turkey who believes he is an eagle'. However, he has written a book called *The Extinction of Pauperism* and actually wants to eliminate poverty by giving workers factory ownership."

"So he is really one of us, eh, Father."

"In a way, yes, for a Frenchie - he has even met Charles Dickens. He returned to France at the beginning of the 1848 revolutions, crossing paths on the way with the deposed king, Louis Philippe, who came here to exile. But he returned later to London to observe events in France and after the Revolution became first a member of the National Assembly, then President, by popular vote. He is actually Britain's ally, liked and supported by Victoria.

"Why doesn't the Turkish sultan forbid anyone to interfere in his empire?"

"He's too weak – Turkey is 'the sick man of Europe' and Russia hopes to see it disintegrate and claims protection of fifteen million Greek Orthodox Christians, just as Napoleon III supports Roman Catholics in the Holy Land, including Jerusalem's Church of the Holy Sepulchre. The Russians say they have invaded the principalities to 'protect' Christians, but the French have allied with England to try and stop him interfering."

William, now eighteen, had noticed that Britain's new Militia was growing rapidly, attracting men who wanted military experience, while maintaining their civilian jobs and family life. He liked the idea of receiving basic training at a local army depot at weekends while continuing civilian life, so he could decide what he finally wanted: there was even an annual camp, including time on the rifle ranges: it seemed like a holiday.

He discussed his intentions with his older brother, Christopher, who thought he was mad, but the Crimean War gave William a possible aim, warped though it seemed – to defend the Sultan against creeping Tsarist colonialism in Europe. Militia regiments were offering to fund passages out to the Crimea, so he decided to join as soon as he was old enough.

He followed the war in the newspapers and continued to question Father:

"Why, Father, are we are on the side of Muslim, rather than Christian Russia?"

"You have to understand, son, that this is more political than religious - it is not a crusade: The Tsar has his eyes on Turkish land and talks about "the sick man of Europe" which he wants to steal from the Ottoman Empire, including Egypt and Crete, which England also wants. The Russian envoy in Turkey, Prince Mentchikoff, is making arrogant claims for an Imperial protectorate over the Christian population of Turkey, which is why we support Turkey. Stratford de Redcliffe, our Ambassador, wants war. Russia is now constructing a huge fortified dockyard at Sebastopol in the Crimea to challenge British control of the seas and that is why the English fleet is moving towards the Dardanelles."

"So much for the success of Prince Albert's peaceful Great Exhibition of all the Works of all the Nations, Father."

On the 4th October, the Sultan, encouraged by British and French support, declared war on Russia when they refused to leave Turkish territory in Europe; and two weeks later, the Allied fleets entered the Dardanelles.

Turkish troops were able to vanquish the Russians in Moldavia and Wallachia, with welcome Austrian neutrality and William was sympathetic to the rapid build-up of British Enthusiasm for war, encouraged by the newspapers.

Unlike Britain's rational Prime Minister Aberdeen - and William's Pleasley vicar - William became intoxicated by the prospect of war. Russia was the enemy and Turkey an "industrious and brave friend", religion apart - it was inconvenient, but political brotherhood was more important. William supported the British Press's pro-Turkish jingoism.

On 30th November, when he read about the tragic sinking of ten wooden patrol ships by Russian incendiary shells at the battle of Sinope, he agreed with the British press descriptions of a "foul outrage" and "massacre": also that "never, in naval warfare was so horrifying slaughter ever witnessed. Five thousand sailors prevented from swimming ashore by Russia grape and canister."

"Five thousand murders," William kept muttering, more determined than ever to join the army when he reached the age of twenty-one, though he did not then divulge his murderous thoughts to the Pleasley vicar, or his father.

He would learn only later in life that this was also the usual disproportionately bloodthirsty British way with enemies in India, Africa and the Sudan, but being very young, whooped for joy when the House of Commons decided on the destruction of Sebastopol by patrolling the Black sea and making the Russians stay in port.

The British papers were full of it:

God's just wrath shall be wreaked on a giant liar and by attacking Sebastopol, we have proved we have hearts in a cause, we are noble still.

William quickly adopted this pseudo-religious self-righteousness when, on 28th March 1854, Britain and France declared war - his birthday. He whooped with joy when Russia ordered the withdrawal from Wallachia and Moldavia two months later and agreed with the Home Sec, Palmerston's wanting to make "an example of the red-haired barbarians" and promote anti-Russian feeling

 "Well, it may mean the Russians have their eyes on Afghanistan and our India. There is also tension over the Holy Places in Palestine, which are controlled by Turkey: the Russian Orthodox Church wants them and so does the new Emperor, Napoleon III of France."

"We surely don't want another war with France, Father."

"No, son, the new Napoleon is very friendly. He came here after laughable failures at revolution in France, the year after you were born. We have nothing to fear from him: though he is trying to imitate his famous uncle, he is really only 'a turkey who believes he is an eagle'. However, he has written a book called *The Extinction of Pauperism* and actually wants to eliminate poverty by giving workers factory ownership."

"So he is really one of us, eh, Father."

"In a way, yes, for a Frenchie - he has even met Charles Dickens. He returned to France at the beginning of the 1848 revolutions, crossing paths on the way with the deposed king, Louis Philippe, who came here to exile. And he returned later to London to observe events in France, though after the Revolution, he became first a member of the National Assembly, then president by popular vote. He is actually Britain's ally, liked and supported by Victoria.

"Why doesn't the Turkish sultan forbid anyone to interfere in his empire?"

"He's too weak – Turkey is 'the sick man of Europe' and Russia hopes to see it disintegrate and claims protection of fifteen million Greek Orthodox Christians, just as Napoleon III supports Roman Catholics in Turkey's Holy Land, including Jerusalem's Church of the Holy Sepulchre. The Russians say they have invaded the principalities to 'protect' Christians and the French have allied with England to try and stop him interfering."

As England prepared its army, William was angry when, during another Commons debate, Disraeli said Britain was "going to war to prevent Russia protecting the Christian subjects" and "the Tsar was right when he called us the enemies of Christianity". William thought this very unpatriotic for a Jewish MP.

The war was so popular that, like most, William did not complain when income tax rose from seven pence to one-shilling-and-two pence. As troops started crossing the Sea of Marmara for the Scutari barracks and Constantinople, William wished he could be there with them.

For the next months, William followed the war, impatient to join up in March, 1855 on his twenty-first birthday. He was disgusted to read about the neglected state of the British army, which had not seen action since the Napoleonic Wars and negative reports from the war reporter, William Russell, who criticised the British Commanders as useless.

Lord Raglan, C-in-C, aged sixty-six, had once been on Wellington's staff, but had seen no active service since Waterloo (1815) where he had lost his arm - and nearly his wedding ring. He was tactful and good tempered, but kept referring to his French allies as 'the enemy'. Lord Lucan was fifty-four and had bought the 17th Lancers for £25,000. He made them into dandies and had never seen action himself. His brother-in-law, Lord Cardigan, fifty-seven, who led the Light Brigade had also seen no active service - an arrogant snob, a scandalous upper class hooligan who had paid £40,000 to command the 11th Hussars. He was a grotesque specimen of aristocratic eccentricity who was to lead the stupidly-courageous Charge of the Brigade.

Soldiers clothing was unsuitable for the changeable Crimean climate and their knapsacks weighed 30lb. Britain's 30,000 troops were catered for from Whitehall by medics and Ordnance, which meant that Raglan had no control over them and there were no transport or medical services in the field. To make matters worse, thousands of boots were destroyed by fire Varna, or lost in storms. Supply was a disaster

William later learnt from William Russell's reports that Allied forces had immediately begun to deteriorate through drunkenness, and in Scutari, at least 2,400 men were reported one night to be in brothels and taverns, where they attacked their fellow Turks. Self-inflicted harm became a chief cause of the high mortality.

For the moment, however, William cheered when the Allied fleet bombarded Odessa, though he was disgusted when he learned the Cabinet were asleep when the Invasion of Crimea was announced in August. At home, for want of the truth, optimism prevailed: "We've got the men, we've got the ships, we've got the money, too," lied popular Palmerston, while the unpopular peace-loving Prime Minister, Aberdeen, was pictured as an old woman blacking the Tsar's boots!

Soon, cholera spread round the British first landing spot of Varna in Anatolia: terrified soldiers were slavering at the mouth, crying out and clutching their bellies, falling, crawling, or in a stupor. There was a total absence of drugs and five thousand perished in a few days.

Partly through ignorance, William paid little attention to these conditions, dreaming all the time of 'action', sympathising with the soldiers at the front who wanted to know where the Russians were. He thought the decision to invade the Crimea a good chance to teach the Russians a lesson by capturing the naval base of Sebastopol, which was threatening England's sea power.

William followed events from the landing at Kalamita Bay, north of Sebastopol, in terribly-changeable weather for which the British were ill-dressed, suffering many deaths from cholera - one of the reasons Raglan wanted to get out of Varna and find the enemy. But the Crimea was a huge risk, with no railways and an unpredictable climate, though William was not in the least deterred by this plan.

Despite incompetence, dis-organisation and disease (mostly cholera and dysentery), he read joyfully how the British had managed to land on the Crimea and make a beachhead four miles inland, before turning south and fighting their first successful battle at Alma on 20th September 1854, thirty-five miles north of Sevastopol.

The Russians made a stand on the heights above the south bank of the Alma, where a mere three battalions of the Highland Brigade Led by Sir Colin Campbell, advanced in a dangerously thin red line, two hundred yards long, which the Russians were unable to see was only two ranks deep. The Brigade advanced while firing, a difficult task, and the road to Sevastopol was now open.

William was overjoyed to read this news and now impatient to go out and was thrilled when he read Campbell words to his men, the 93rd Highlanders: "you must die where you stand". Cardigan, looking on, had jealously muttered, "damn those heavies!".

But delays and a split Anglo-French command, with men dying at twenty-five a day and the approach of a terrible winter, meaning an attack on Sebastopol was abandoned. By 27th October, William read that the Allies were camped to the south at Balaklava and bombarding Sebastopol.

He now regularly read William Russell's reports in the *Times* newspaper and learned that whereas the French lived comparatively well, both British officers and men lived in tented squalor, wearing the remnants of their summer uniforms and spending long hours in trenches, day after day exposed to cold and rain. With no communal cooking, every man had to fend for himself, find his own water and firewood in areas now stripped bare of every twig. And with no latrines, the camp became a filthy quagmire, full of rats and lice, leading to disease. The organisation of supplies from England collapsed, due to the necessity of filling in so many forms.

But William was thrilled to learn of the charge of Lord Cardigan's Light Brigade, though it was a total blunder caused by vague, misunderstood orders - according to the Poet Laureate it was still glorious, though the "soldier knew someone had blundered".

And in trench warfare, the army was neglected, while disease continued apace - sixty thousand allies pitched against one hundred thousand Russians, where rain and mist made for much confusion and tiredness. Along with most of the English, William continued unfairly to criticise the Prime Minister Aberdeen's apparent lack of concern for the sufferings of ordinary soldiers.

During the terrible winter of 1854-5 and failure at Inkerman, ordinary English people became so infuriated by the mismanagement that they began raising money for medicine and stores and knitting warm caps. At work, William was asked for money by his managers, while his mother, like Queen Victoria, knitted soldiers' mittens for the vicious Crimean winter: meanwhile, troops soaked in trenches, hospital tents blew down and high winds made moving objects dangerous.

Yet it was still better to die in the trenches than go to hospital, where conditions were awful, till the arrival of angelic Florence Nightingale showed what compassion, organisation and cleanliness could do with fifty percent of the army sick.

William was appalled to learn how many British ships sank in the harbour and provisions lost and it was galling to read how much better the French were looked after.

William Russell opened William's eyes to the disaster for soldiers in the British Army and he was unsympathetic to Prince Albert's anger at the "pen and ink of one miserable scribbler in despoiling the country", and Victoria's talk of Russell's "infamous attacks against our army, which have disgraced our newspapers". Raglan, whom Russell had described as "utterly incompetent to lead the army", accused him of betraying secrets to the enemy, which concerned William. But as he learned of the appalling state of the Army, William sided with Russell's judgement on the importance of doing something to put it right.

By 1855, Aberdeen's government was moribund, as Russell reported on its apathy, mismanagement and misrule. Mary Secole and Florence Nightingale were the only lights in a very dark tunnel of despair and William was delighted to read that at Balaclava and Scutari, Nightingale improved administration and cleanliness with her "masculine mind", so that the death rate fell from forty-four to two percent in six months"

On 21 January, 1855, William learned of the "snowball riot" in Trafalgar Square in which one-thousand-five-hundred people had protested against the war by pelting buses, cabs, and pedestrians with snow balls. When the police intervened, they, too were pelted. The riot was put down by police with truncheons.

But Aberdeen had written wisely to Russell about the pointlessness of all wars:

"The abstract justice of the cause, although indisputable, is but a poor consolation for the inevitable calamities of all war, or for a decision which I am not without fear may prove to have been impolitic and unwise. My conscience upbraids... because it is possible that by a little more energy and vigour, not on the Danube, but in Downing Street, it might have been prevented."

William thought this a cowardly thing to have written; the only person who agreed with Aberdeen was William's pacifist local vicar. After the battle of Balaklava, Tory MP's had demanded adequate accounting of all soldiers, cavalry and sailors sent to the Crimea, and accurate casualty figures sustained. William was relieved when Aberdeen resigned in January and Palmerston, the anti-Russian, became PM at the age of seventy.

He then hoped things would slowly begin to improve, supporting Palmerston's hard line to foment unrest inside the Russian Empire. It would take time for things to be put right, but the April 9th English attack on the Sebastopol Redan was a disaster.

When William read in July of despondency and moral deterioration through cholera and incompetent officers like Lucan, Cardigan and Airey, he finally decided finally to join up. He would take a train to York to train with the 7th Hussars – the very regiment that had cruelly put down the peaceful demonstration at Peterloo in 1819. He was not fully aware that in the Crimea many young raw recruits sickened and died within weeks, falling asleep in their tents and never waking up; or that by February 1855 British fighting strength had fallen to a mere twelve thousand.

Mrs Duberly, whose husband was in William's future regiment described his future destination of Balaklava thus:

Take a village of ruined houses and hovels in the extremist state of all imaginable dirt; allow the rain to pour into and outside them, until the whole place is a swamp of filth ankle-deep; catch about – on average - a thousand Turks with the plague and cram them into the houses indiscriminately; kill about a hundred a day and bury them so as to be scarcely covered with earth, leaving them to rot at leisure-taking care, to keep up the supply. Onto one part of the beach drive all the exhausted baggage ponies, dying bullocks, and worn-out camels and leave them to die of starvation. They will generally do so in about three days, when they will soon begin to rot and smell accordingly. Collect together from the water of the harbour all the offal of the animals slaughtered for the use of the occupants of above one hundred ships, to say nothing of the inhabitants of the town – which, together with all an occasional floating human body, whole of in parts, and the driftwood of the wrecks, pretty well covers the water – and stew them all up together in a narrow harbour and you will have a tolerable imitation of the real essence of Balaklava.

Admittedly, this was before things began to improve - before William's arrival at the end of the war, when huts began to arrive and measures were taken to reorganise distribution and sanitation; when a railway line from Balaklava to the front was begun and by March a drainage system was installed in

Scutari. Balaklava harbour was cleared, though by the time winter uniforms arrived, it was too hot to wear them.

William's Hussars were light cavalry: fast, but hard-hitting troops for reinforcement, or breaking enemy flanks. Formerly the 7th Queen's Own Light Dragoons, the old armoured infantry trained to fight both on foot (usually in reconnaissance) and on horseback (in bigger battles). They became Hussars in 1807, when the Prince Regent made radical alterations to the uniforms.

What would William's family think of his decision to fight after the local vicar's conversation, who agreed with Lord Aberdeen's right to say war was a disgraceful act of insanity to all concerned? He had also thought the Tsar right to protest when Napoleon III had wanted to force the Turks to give France the keys to the Church in Bethlehem.

The vicar had argued that if France and Britain hadn't promised each other support, the Ottomans wouldn't have declared war on Russia in October 1853 and the Russian fleet wouldn't have destroyed the Turkish fleet at Sinope, so, in turn, England wouldn't have sent forces to Gallipoli to attack Russia.

"It has come to something when we have to attack a fellow-Christian country and defend heathen Muslims," he said.

William, now eighteen, had noticed Britain's new Militia was growing rapidly, attracting men wanting military experience, while at the same time maintaining their civilian jobs and family life. He liked the idea of receiving basic training at a local army depot at weekends while continuing civilian life: there was even an annual camp, with time on the rifle range and it seemed like a holiday.

He discussed his intentions with his peace-loving older brother, Christopher, who thought he was mad, but the Crimean War gave William a possible aim – a military career defending the Turkish Sultan against creeping Tsarist colonialism in Europe. Joining a Militia regiment also offered funding for a passage out to the Crimea, so William decided to join as soon as he was old enough.

He still continued questioning his Father while following foreign policy in the newspapers:

"Why, Father, are we are on the side of Muslim Turkey, rather than Christian Russia?"

"You have to understand, son, that this war is more political than religious - it is not a crusade: the Tsar has his eyes on Turkish land and talks about "the sick man of Europe" in order to steal it. This includes Egypt and Crete, which England also wants. The Russian envoy in Turkey, Prince Mentchikoff, is making arrogant claims for an Imperial protectorate over the Christian population of Turkey, which is why we support Turkey. Stratford de Redcliffe, our

Ambassador, wants war and Russia is now constructing a huge fortified dockyard at Sebastopol in the Crimea to challenge British control of the seas, which is why the English fleet is moving towards the Dardanelles."

"So much for Prince Albert's peaceful Great Exhibition of all the Works of all the Nations, Father."

On 4th October, the Sultan, encouraged by British and French support, declared war on Russia after they refused to leave Turkish territory in Europe; two weeks later, the Allied fleets entered the Dardanelles. Thankfully, Turkish troops were able to vanquish the Russians in Moldavia and Wallachia, with welcome Austrian neutrality.

William was very sympathetic to the rapid build-up of British enthusiasm for war, encouraged by the newspapers - unlike Britain's rational Prime Minister Aberdeen - and William's Pleasley vicar. His youthful exuberance became intoxicated by the prospect of war: Russia was his enemy and Turkey an industrious and brave friend. True, the Sultan's religion was inconvenient, but political brotherhood was more important.

On 30th November, William read about the tragic sinking of ten wooden patrol ships by Russian incendiary shells at the battle of Sinope, and agreed with the British press descriptions of a "foul outrage" and "massacre": also that "never, in naval warfare was so horrifying slaughter ever witnessed – five thousand sailors prevented from swimming ashore by grape and canister."

"Five thousand murders," William kept muttering, more determined than ever to join the army when he reached the age of twenty-one, though he did not yet divulge these thoughts to the Pleasley vicar, or his father.

He would learn only later in life that this "foul outrage" was the usual disproportionately bloodthirsty British way with its enemies in India, Africa and the Sudan, but he was very young and whooped for joy when the House of Commons decided on the destruction of Sebastopol by patrolling the Black sea to make the Russians stay in port.

The papers were full of it:

God's just wrath shall be wreaked on a giant liar and by attacking Sebastopol, we have proved we have hearts in a cause, we are noble still.

William quickly adopted this pseudo-religious self-righteousness when, on 28th March 1854, Britain and France declared war on his birthday. He whooped with joy when Russia ordered withdrawal from Wallachia and Moldavia two months later and agreed with the Home Sec, Palmerston wanting to make "an example of the red-haired barbarians" and promote anti-Russian feeling

He took a final decision, hatched since his sixteenth birthday, by signing up for the Militia, hoping the war would not be over before he was twenty-one and old enough to join up. He was still working at the mill, but was given time off to train in the use of the new Minie rifles, with conical-cylindrical soft lead bullets and three exterior grease-filled grooves. This French invention provided spin for accuracy, consistent velocity and longer range, causing huge wounds with larger sized bullets. It allowed two to three shots a minute and rapid muzzle loading.

William later explained his wish to join the army thus: "I was possessed with a spirit of adventure, not unmixed with a little dare-devilment" and volunteered for the 8th Hussars, having had had some previous military training: his regimental number – 1564 - meant he was sent straight to the Crimea, rather than to regimental the depot at Newbridge in Ireland for more training.

"Here, here!" said Father, temporarily agreeing with his son and thinking of Pleasley's greedy, mill-owning millionaires. This new Victorian age put wealth above morals, or the health of his working class. But where was the vicar's argument in favour of defending Russia leading?

The vicar continued, "Some people think God's law and the new economics are one, but I disagree. We Christians do not march, as some would have us believe, with Adam Smith's *Wealth of Nations* in one hand and the Sermon on the Mount in the other – they are incompatible, just as defending the Turks against the Russians will weaken our faith. You only have to look at the terrible poverty our capitalism is causing and I do not agree with our church's support of the new workhouses, nor their accusations of lazy immorality on the part of those who succumb to poverty because they "deserve" to. Protestantism should not lead to capitalism because capitalism is selfish: market laws cannot replace a caring home and what it stands for. Today people forget that the pursuit of wealth is not the end of society, but a means to an end: the betterment of all, rather than rewards for the rich."

"And then," said Father, "there is that Darwin fellow, who says we are descended from apes. That can't be good for the Bible message, can it vicar? Not to mention how we are now denied free will in this new materialist doctrine of JS Mill's Utilitarianism. Religion is under attack from all sides. We don't have free will anymore!"

"People are now being led to think the design of the universe does not need God – that it could have happened on its own through scientific laws, like natural selection, with no need of God Almighty. God has been undermined, as with questions of war and peace in the Crimea."

Though liking what the vicar had to say about capitalism, William thought the vicar had failed to appreciate Russia's motives, nor its threat to the

British Empire. He also feared Father might agree with the vicar and oppose his wish to fight, but hoped he would be sympathetic because of his love of horses. On the other hand, father would certainly not like the idea of the inevitable killing these lovely creatures with canon. William therefore planned to appease his father by promising to guard them with his life with an innocent appeal which would ignore the obvious truth about the cruelty of war.

William felt strongly that though hours in his Pleasley "prison" mill had been reduced, Jeremy Bentham's idea of counting happiness as if it were mathematical units by adding up facts could not explain human motives like happiness – for example, in military service, or defence of an idea. And JS Mill wrongly thought things would incrementally improve for everybody under capitalism, believing that free markets and production could be for the greatest good – possibly because he was a silly aristocratic optimist who had never worked in his life and had no idea how selfish the mill owners really were.

But William had to be careful how he broached the subject of leaving home. When they were settled at home after work next day, William began by criticising factory work:

"We only providing money for the wealthy, while we work like slaves. Look what PM Russell did when workers presented their perfectly reasonable Charter a few years ago - crushed on Kennington Common, simply for listening to speakers. I want to serve my country and see the world."

"Yes, son, but you want to volunteer for a questionable war, which is going badly for us, with lots of pointless killing, most of which is caused by disease, despite lovely Florence Nightingale. Your Christianity ought to tell you this is not glorious, but wrong."

William knew that at some stage Father would drag God into it and gave his real opinion on the subject for the first time.

"I think God – the universal spirit - is mystical nonsense. History should be studied by looking at what is actually happening, like in this war, not what people hope will happen in a future life when they are dead."

"You'll be telling me next the Bible is useless mythology and that Charles Darwin was right when he said we are all monkeys."

"Father, you cannot explain the knowable in terms of the unknowable. You have to study society and find rational explanations. This chap Karl Marx may have a point: my cotton factory cannot change without reasoned revolution."

The vicar now rejoined the conversation:

"I tell you, son, the factory keeps this family alive, and England has become great round the world through its commerce and trade. Revolution would ruin all that!"

"But father, our factory owns me and I want free of it."

"I see." Father's voice softened.

"I want out. I have given my notice and will stop work at the end of the week. I have decided to fight for Britain against the Russians, for the principle of Turkish national sovereignty against Russia."

"What? Fight for British aristocrats and capitalists, whom you hate and want to overthrow? This is idealism gone mad. Where do you think you will end up? Dead by Cholera or bullets! A marvellous escape from work at Pleasey!"

"I'm sorry, Father."

"Have you talked to Mother?"

"Not yet, but I have mentioned it to my sisters."

"What did they say?"

"They said 'it's my choice, but be careful'."

"Well, all I can say is God help you re-think this hasty decision. And do think of your mother."

"Father, please stop bringing God into our conversation. God is nothing but an invention inside each man's head, which the church uses to control us."

"Don't be disrespectful, son. It will upset your mother. You do not know what you are saying."

"Marx says the class war is forced on us by selfish capitalists. I do not want to become a slave: I am joining the army to discover myself and see the world."

"Son, you will never get rid of class. It is the natural way the world works – some are born great, but most obey. So long as we earn enough to live, then we should be happy. Many are a lot poorer than us and this talk of freeing all mankind is exaggerated nonsense."

"Yes, father, but we must work within the logic of history to gain our freedom. Our British philosophical radicals want us to practise moral restraint, even when we are starving – ask us to be prudent when we are exploited. We should be demanding what is rightfully ours as the fruit of our labours. The *Economist* opposed the 1848 Public Health Act on the grounds that suffering and evil are natural and cannot be got rid of; it said that legislation produces more evil than good - stupid journal! It even praised the government for criticising the Bill stopping children working more than ten hours a day – ten hours! And it also rejects elementary education because it might damage our morals and character by teaching us to despise our lot as servants. So much for prudence and sobriety, Father!"

"But son, apart from the rights and wrongs of the Crimean war, the regiment you are joining was the one which put down the Peterloo protesters – murderers to a man! Things are gradually improving, mark my words. All my family work at Pleasley and live reasonably well. There's so much demand because of our empire and plenty of work on the new machines, though many eat only potatoes and oatmeal, though rarely ever milk or meat."

William was afraid his father would mention this inconvenient fact, and tried to sidestep, "But look how mill work breaks up the family with mothers in the factory and husbands at home doing women's work – it's not natural. Children grow up wild without mother for twelve or thirteen hours a day. No wonder there are so many accidents round here – burning, drowning, falling. No one to look after them and no one to feed them when left at home. Capitalism is dissolving the family before our very eyes."

"At least they are earning – better than sitting around doing nothing all day."

William was now on his own young hobby horse, "And you are forgetting the worst part of putting men and women together in confined spaces in factories without moral guidance: the mill language is indecent – filthy - and affects uneducated children. I would rather my daughters begged than work in a factory. Three quarters of pour factory women are unchaste - capitalists want cheap labour, not good morals, Dad."

""But things have improved with the factory acts? Once, five-year-olds worked fourteen to sixteen hours a day and their injuries could be terrible – bent legs, crippled hips, unable to walk upstairs. Fined if they sat – six penny fines for pregnant women sitting down for a rest - in poor ventilation and cotton dust air!"

"Look at me, Father, a spinner: pale and thin from youth, enfeebled, morbid, depressed. I am bored! The endless rattling of machinery is driving me mad. And doors close ten minutes after work starts, or I am fined three pennies, the same if I leave my machine while it is in motion. There is summary dismissal without reason, no talking, singing or whistling. The truck system's goods sold on credit have high prices and benefit only the employers. We are no better than slaves:

There is a king and a ruthless King

Not a king of the poet's dream;

But a tyrant fell, white slaves know well

And that ruthless king is steam."

Father could only repeat, "Have patience, son, things will improve," adding, "at least we are more civilised than the poor Irish. They go in rags, eat potatoes, and sleep in stables, hutches and pig-sties. They drink their wages away and neglect their children."

This angered William,

"That's because their wages are forced down to the lowest on which they and their family can subsist. Employers keep them in an unemployed reserve of workers for the liveliest months of production. When not working they have to beg, steal and survive as best they can till they are needed again in the factories. It is not their fault.

"The famine has reduced them to African slaves, taking lower wages to compete with us Englishmen, which forces us against one another, when we should be united in supporting our needs together. These impoverished beggars compete with us, a million of them every year in our great cities – there are forty thousand in Manchester! They migrate for four pence to England on a steamship packed like cattle and are forced to live anywhere."

"But," said Father, "when not eating potatoes, they drink, my boy. With squalid homes and few clothes, what do they want with high wages? Their filth poisons the air and their pigs sleep with them, as the Arabs love their horses. Being unaccustomed to furniture, they crowd into single rooms, revelling in drink to the point of bestial drunkenness, like savages."

Father was on one of his Irish hobby horses, so William let the matter drop.

But the di was cast: he would go to the Crimea.

Off to the Crimea

William had already volunteered for the Militia, so he did not have to do any extra training and could depart for the Crimea immediately. After tearful goodbyes to mother, father and sisters (his brother was not at home), he was despatched from Southampton in the *Great Britain*, one of three troop ships.

He soon noticed how his fellow soldiers had rapidly acquiring a taste for two gills, or half a pint, of rum, given to the soldiers every day and, for the moment resisted, on Christian principle. his canvas hammock was a generous eighteen inches wide - rather than the usual fourteen - with blanket and his military overcoat for extra warmth.

The weather was breezy round the Bay of Biscay and William soon found there was little to look at except seagulls and fellow-soldiers smoking their pipes, while hoping they would not fall sea-sick. William did not succumb, partly because he was too excited, but also because he was a natural sailor.

He soon discovered he had joined up for same reasons as his fellow soldiers: patriotism, poverty, boredom, a quest for adventure and a wish to see the world. As his fellow-Nottinghamshire friend put it, "Th'as only got one life, so use it!" No-one, however, talked about wanting to die for his country.

The boat stopped at Malta, before reaching the Sea of Gallipoli three weeks after the fall of Sebastopol on 28th September.

"Just our flippin' luck," William remarked to a farmer from near Bolsover, "With Sebastopol gone, the war's over. And yet it feels like only yesterday when the Grenadier and Coldstream Guards marched in slow time to Buckingham Palace at the start of the war. What on earth have we bin doin' in the meantime?"

"Aye and most did not return, thanks to Aberdeen's lousy government," replied his farmer friend.

They then went below-deck for food – beef, with huge quantities of flour and small portions of plums, excellent bread and pea soup, not to mention a half gill of rum, which William had gingerly begun to try, with half a pint of water.

William nudged his fellow and said, *sotto voce*, "have you noticed the sailor who served us is giving more to his fellow-sailors than us soldiers?" The Sergeant Major soon put a stop to it by taking over the grog! – "men, two steps to the front and swallow". They laughed.

'The finest army that has ever left these shores' was now in much better shape, thanks to recent government reforms resulting from previous disasters. William was paid a shilling a day, plus 1d beer money. But his fancy red Hussar uniform up to the collar, was unsuited to tropical climes.

The following day, sea sickness struck and soldiers' heads hung despondently over the side of their creaking, swaying hulk. William – unusually - was now heartily sick, but next day, when the men mustered for prayers, they had all recovered and after ten days reached Malta, to be joined by French troops with distinctive blue uniforms. The British politely saluted foreign officers and the soldiers communicated in sign language.

The four-day voyage to the shelter of the Dardanelles was uneventful, so William now joined the men's eating and drinking, followed by walking on deck, before resuming the same. There was also singing from various regiments, to great applause.

When the ship anchored next day, a boat came from shore with interpreters and William learned that cavalry horses were nowhere to be found, provisions were expensive and the French had taken all the best lodgings because they had come to the Crimea first. They seemed much better organised than the English, so perhaps little had changed from Russell's previous dire war reports.

One old soldier, just returned from leave, told them they were lucky the situation had improved: "When I first arrived at the beginning of the war, there were no preparations to receive the troops, and no interpreters. We had to give up our homes to the

French, and move up hill, where the Greeks hated us. British officials had no plans or foresight when they sent us out. What is more, the officers demanded and were given first choice with animals, digs and provisions."

"Aye," pitched in a Scotsman, "we had no beds at all and only the single regulation blanket, so we had to do things in reverse: dress to go to bed, putting on all our spare clothing. Worse, the sick from Malta had to stay in the cold camp with one blanket and no hospital provisions."

"But," replied the old soldier, "we couldn't grumble because our officers were dressed as badly as we were – old patched coats and boots. They marched beside us, slept by us, fought and died with us.

"And the weather of 1854-5 was God-awful. At Inkerman, it rained incessantly, and the fog was so thick we could not see two yards in front of us" – he spat over the side of the boat before resuming – "the bloodiest struggle ever witnessed since war cursed this earth. Masses of men resisted the bayonet again and again as the Russians charged with incredible fury – all in vapours and foggy drizzle, so we could not tell where the enemy was."

William and the new soldiers were all ears: he was now hearing what it was really like for the first time.

"On 14th July last year we suffered a hurricane," continued his friend, "pelting rain and streams of water under our tents that saturated blankets. The rain was followed by rushing, howling wind over the common, and our tents flapped till the pegs began to loosen and driving rain entered the tents right into our faces."

The old soldier took up the story, "Soon tent poles bent like straw - cracked like glass - and tents came down, till we were pressed down and half stifled by heavy folds of wet canvas.

"Outside, the whole camp was beaten flat to earth and we chased through mud in all directions, after our clothes and personal effects. The air was filled with blankets, hats and greatcoats - even tables and chairs - before trying to make our way – wounded, too - to windowless, roofless barns for shelter.

"Do you remember," he asked of no-one in particular, part of Lord Raglan's roof was carried off, wagons overturned, men and horses knocked down, half of our cavalry horses let loose. Lord Lucan was sitting up to his knees in sludge for hours." His companion laughed. "And Cardigan was sick on board his yacht in Balaklava Bay, along with many generals. Lucky bastards, having ships to go to."

The old soldier continued, "Then it got colder - the wind veered and snow followed. Finally, we got shelter in a barn for our regiment's horses of the 8th Hussars. We were packed like herrings in a barrel till nightfall, when we slept in the straw with our animals for company. We learned that several ships had been lost in Balaklava Bay – driven out of the water and on their sides. The sun came next day, but the roads were quagmires. The rain just kept pouring and the skies were black as ink - tents with one foot of water letting in rain like sieves. A wretched beggar in London led the life of a prince, compared to us."

His companion then cheered William and his friends: "You have just missed a terrible winter - no doubt there will be others – with rations cut for nine days, no issue of tea, coffee or sugar - not to mention ammunition – because of ships sunk and wagons unable to negotiate sodden roads.

"Clothing and food went down with our ships or were saturated by water. We suffered greatly in 1855 because no one in England was responsible for putting things right – cursed as we were by requisitions, orders and memos written by an army of useless scriveners.

"You remember," he said, looking at his friend, "the gallant captain Swinton of the Royal Artillery who was found dead in his tent through suffocation from the fumes of a useless charcoal stove - hundreds bought in Constantinople were no good."

His friend agreed by spitting on the sod.

"And Christmas was so dreary! No presents from our loved ones because they had been sunk - or pilfered. There were three-thousand-five-hundred soldiers sick in the British camp before Sebastopol. Where were our new huts? Still on board ships in Balaklava, or used for firewood. Roads clogged with dead horses.

"The French, however, were alright", continued William's companion sarcastically. "Would you believe – a French officer invited me into his warm tent where there was a case of Bordeaux, a box of brandy and a pile of tobacco sent by Napoleon III – their soldiers' greatest friend - while we were stuck with anti-social Lucan, who cared nothing for the ordinary soldier."

"Thankfully, the weather has now changed for the better," ended the soldier's informative conversation. He added, "you, my friends, are a new generation: the old army has passed away with wounds, sickness or death. Only Raglan and Lucan remain."

"Thank god William Russell told the truth in his articles and reforms took place," thought William, gratefully.

His companion continued, "The weather has improved, but cholera continues – just like the end of November 1854 and the beginning of the war - with a dreadful violence. I remember a day in Varna when six hundred Frenchmen lay dead. Frightful! They were convinced there was something in the air. The whole camp was like a terrible hospital. Awful barracks – windows broken, walls cracked and shaky, floors mouldering and rotten. The smell was abominable: the men were frequently attacked with cholera and rapidly died. After that, we were more than happy to decamp for the Crimea. But of course, Cholera came with us."

His companion took up the story, "Many men went reckless, verging on madness. They could be seen lying drunk in the ditches by the road side, under the blazing sun, covered with swarms of flies, eating themselves stupid with cucumbers, water melons and pears, before returning to their brandy. Varna was a death trap."

William asked the captain where they were bound exactly and learned that his regiment were intended for Scutari, opposite Istanbul, to the south of the Bosphorus, which, he learned meant *ox ford* - now famous for the work of Florence Nightingale, who had done so much to improve the life chances of sick soldiers.

Mary Seacole had also offered to help but Victorian racism had prevented her, so she moved nearer the front to entertain and provide for soldiers on a personal level.

William soon learned that in Scutari and dirty Constantinople, you could 'get drunk for sixpence and syphilis for a shilling'. His old soldier friends now finished their story of their first journey out to the Crimea:

"Disease broke out even after we left Malta which, my friends, you will find kills more than bullets."

Another soldier bitterly told William, "We were sent to defend a rotten cause and a Turkish race that almost every Christian despises, but it didn't matter because we soldiers have nothing to do with politics".

William began to think about the link between fighting and politics and came, finally, to understood he was a mere slave to his British political masters - nine-hundred-thousand were to die, but he could not see how the Crimean war connected to his Pleasley Mill and poverty in England? Had he made a bad mistake and was his vicar right?

Then - fortunately – came news of the fall of Sebastopol after the British disaster of the Redan with its two-thousand-five-hundred casualties, beginning with a massive four-day bombardment on August 17th. But even in September the city continued under constant fire from the northern shore, so that engineers destroying the docks were shot at and no ships could dock in the harbour.

William stepped ashore at Balaklava on 28th September, 1855, having travelled for 28 days on *The Great Britain*. The war being over, his regiment was sent away from the Crimea so as avoid the terrible conditions of the previous winter. They camped at Ismid (Smyrna).

Now the war was over before William could take part in it, despite all his excitement in watching its progress from England. He was now stationed in Scutari, to avoid another terrible winter and on 7th November in Ismid (ancient Nicomedia) at the entrance to the Black Sea –'a wretched Turkish town in wood with very narrow streets.'

He was hospitalised from 15th-31st March, 1855 with a stomach complaint – "cholera", he would joke – and after that, in anti-climax, his regiment was sent home on 23rd April (St. George's Day), a month after the armistice. His war had been little more than sight-seeing and listening to tales. Finally, he took Steam ship from Liverpool for Dublin on 16th May.

William had been very lucky and could answer no direct questions about the war because he hadn't really been there, but Russell's *Times* had shattered patriotic complacency and, despite final victory, people were looking for a scapegoat in the richest country in the world, where incompetent officers had been appointed from interest, rather than suitable skills.

HOME

On 12th May 1856, William's Hussars arrived back in Portsmouth to be inspected by the Queen, and he saw Albert and The Princess Royal give a low bow. He also saw Fanny Duberly, last seen around camp in the Crimea accompanying her husband. She was shortly to produce a famous book on her adventures.

How beautiful seemed the English countryside that May! William was now on leave and stayed with his Mother at Pleasley Vale, discussing the Treaty of Paris of March, 1856. The vicar of Pleasley was invited by Mother to welcome William home and eagerly wanted to know what the Crimea was like after all the negative accounts he had read in the papers.

William was able to reassure him that "though things had earlier been as bad as reported, they had got much better towards the end – discipline, provisions, food and medicine had all improved. Thank god I missed the worst part!"

"Thank god you missed all the action and arrived too late," added Mother, overjoyed to see her son, though fearing he might want stay in the army for the perverse reasons that only men harboured.

The vicar continued the discussion, "Our government thinks the peace is too lenient and that we should have continued the war to revenge our defeat in the Redan. Why didn't our navy stop them shelling

Sebastopol after it capitulated? What do you think, Christopher?"

"The English now bluster about continuing war, but the Frogs want to sit down and croak in peace, for which I am glad - it was an unnecessary, terrible war."

"But little has changed," added the vicar. "Sebastopol has been restored – alright, it was, after all, part of Russia, though thankfully, the Black Sea has been neutralised and the Danube is now open water. And the principalities have become the new state of Rumania."

The Vicar was displeased there was no mention of the Holy Places – "after all, they were one of the reasons for the war!" He was, however, pleased the Sultan had issued a *firman* to improve conditions of all Christians in his Turkish Empire.

William thought non-militarisation of the Black Sea and neutrality a good thing, though the Treaty was denounced in the Commons as too soft with "nothing to show who was victor and vanquished".

He did, however, complain about the bitter recriminations in Whitehall blaming the army administration and generals for the awful inadequacies earlier in the war. He agreed with William Russell's despatches from the front that these were more the fault of the government than army.

***

William visited London for the victory celebrations, where he saw an allegorical Scutari peace monument at Crystal Palace, a seventy-foot high goddess with garments of silver, a scarf of gold on a base of green marble, with a base of eight life-sized statues. he also enjoyed an exhibition of fireworks in London Parks – though two were killed with rocket sticks and several lost the sight of one eye in the climax of 14,00 rockets. He also witnessed the planting of Crimean crocuses.

In the four years since the new House of Commons was finished, he was duly impressed and thought the £2.5 million pounds well spent. Its medieval style was interesting, though he was not impressed that it was, after Peterloo, a reflection of the continuing power of the British aristocracy over ordinary people. The clock tower would not be completed till 1858, but he noted its position for future reference.

He got rather lost when it was dark and wondered where on earth he was. Two figures approached in top hats and long coats and as they passed, one said jokingly,

"You looking for the workhouse? You look as if you need one!" As they receded, William heard them say, "O why can't the poor just die quietly, rather than increase unnecessary population? I say send them all to the workhouse!"

As they walked towards the huge unfinished gothic building looming out of the mist by the river Thames, the last thing William heard was his being unflatteringly likened to one of Darwin's apes in the new theory of Evolution. Obviously, God and Nature were now at odds in William's new Britain.

He then passed a couple of workmen talking about the new Parliament building they were working on:

"Can't understand why this bloke Charles Barry had to do it in what they are calling Gothic Revival? That's medieval, ain't it?"

"He's deliberately lookin' back because we are going forward too fast. I blame Peel's Free Trade. Back to the future, heh! Heh! He'll go mad eventually."

"Talk about a house on fire!"

"Modern Britain, eh?"

"Ha! Ha!"

William also passed through the London Docks and witnessed poverty even worse than Mansfield's because shipping had not got through and there was little employment. He saw many drunks, trying to numb the impact of poverty by drinking, many children, some already prostitutes for foreign sailors who fought over them, drunk, like their parents.

It struck him once more that this centre of Britain's rich world trade, with its great ships and warehouses containing the great wealth of the globe, should be sustained by the poorest people gaining little from the free trade of wealthy aristocrats and industrialists, who seemed to have joined hands to keep their wealth away from the workers. He was reminded briefly of Karl Marx.

William had had enough of London and wanted to go back home to Pleasley – though not for long: his Crimean adventure had whetted his appetite for adventure, which he was soon to find with the outbreak of the Indian Mutiny in 1857.

THE INDIAN MUTINY

And so, William now returned to Ireland with his regiment, but within months, was back home in Pleasley with family, still in the same jobs, apart from father, now retired from the Vicarage. At fifty-eight, he was ageing fast but mother - in her mid-fifties - was still lively. His sisters, near his own age, save Hannah, twelve years older and brother Christopher, twenty years older, still worked in Pleasley mill.

In 1857, news reached England of an Indian sepoy mutiny, apparently caused by unwise and insensitive use of pork and cow cartridge grease in guns, which offended both Muslim and Hindu religious sensibilities. It didn't seem possible that this alone could have caused a mutiny against British colonial rule, for it was confined mainly to the north and centre and at first people downplayed the danger.

It all began at Dum-Dum (home of the infamous bullets), near Calcutta, after a low cast had apparently told an annoyingly superior Brahmin sepoy that his bullets were greased with pig and cow fat – forbidden in both Muslim and Hindu religions. The British, of course, were arrogant enough to ignore its effects, though they were shortly to regret it.

At nearby Barrackpore, there was distrust of the cartridges and Captain Allen was told of supposed British plot where sepoys were being forced to give up cast and become Christians. It was rumoured that

Mutineers were going to seize Fort William in Calcutta and kill Europeans. Though the commanding officer, General Hearsey, told the men in fluent Hindustani that there was no plot to make Christians, alarm was spreading fast.

He dashed to the native lines to find Mangal Pande, under the influence of an intoxicating drug, with loaded musket, calling on the bugler to get the sepoys to come out against the Europeans, who were, he said, "here, for your religion...From biting cartridges you will become infidels...Get ready...you have incited me to do this, turn out all of you." An English sergeant major demanded to know why Pande had not been arrested, before the latter opened fire, bringing down horse and rider. A sepoy then prevented Pande from killing the wounded English, who made good his escape.

When General Hearsay approached with his musket, Mangal Pandy tried to shoot himself, but did not die and was brought to trial a week later. At twenty-six and in the army for seven years, he admitted to have been under the influence of drugs, but would say no more.

The English had lately noted how the sepoys were sullen and sluggish in their duty, but still held them loyal and faithful. Pandy was executed on 8th April and his 19th regiment were marched from Berhamore to Barrackpore and ordered to pile their arms, before being sent home - six weeks later, to be disarmed and disbanded.

Typically, the old English General Anson did not take a gloomy view of sepoys on the verge of violence, though firing practice was suspended for the moment. Calcutta did not want to abandon it and in future sepoys were told they could tear off the ends of cartridges with their fingers, rather than bite them, but this did not quieten them. Soon after the first firing practice, the bungalows of those who had used the new cartridges were burned down. Who was behind it all?

When William first talked with his father about the threat of war in India, he thought at first it didn't amount to much and would soon pass. Typically, the British Press presented it as a misunderstanding on the part of ignorant Indians, rather than insensitively high-handed British colonialism.

But rumours about a new rifle and heavily-greased cartridge paper continued to spread rapidly. Also, unlike the old days, lack of understanding between British officers and Indian men caused abuse of sepoys by ignorantly racist British who swore at, degraded and laughed at them for their beliefs, whereas in old times, men and officers enjoying social life together: in the eighteenth century, white men had taken Indian wives and they had behaved socially as one.

For this historic reason, though older officers did not believe that trouble would spread, times had changed, so that when sepoys were assured by British officers there was nothing to fear from the cartridges, there was gloomy silence and in Barrackpore, they planned to rise up, burn down their officers' bungalows and kill Europeans. European women were now afraid at the disrespect they were being shown and when strange stories of an unsettled India circulated, the thick-skinned British at last began to sense trouble.

When Brigadier Archdale Wilson returned from Simla to Meerut to hear that the 3rd did not like the new cartridges, he ordered then on parade on 24th April. His officers were warned that the sepoys would not defile themselves with new cartridges unless every other regiment in India did as well.

When ninety men were ordered to take three cartridges and refused, giving no reasons, they were harshly given ten years with hard labour, though they had previously been of good conduct.

On May 9th, William read that all the Meerut troops were assembled on the European infantry parade ground, forming three sides of a square when the convicted men were marched and halted, for their sentence to be read out. They were then stripped of uniforms, boots removed and ankles shackled. Some of them berated fellow-sepoys for not helping them.

Both William and his father thought this unjustifiably harsh and realised something was rotten in the state of British India. As the men went off to jail some threw their boots at the Colonel, cursing him in Hindustani for their complete humiliation, stripped and fettered.

William talked to an old soldier friend just returned from India, who had witnessed unwelcome changes in British attitudes to the Indian.

"All classes are now suspicious. It began at Dum-Dum with the rumours of cartridges smeared in pig and cow fat, even before they actually were – which spread like wild fire. It seems to me the rumours were deliberately exaggerated to make Indians dissatisfied with other things about English rule. The greased cartridge issue was as an excuse for getting at us for other reasons.

"We have already displaced the popular king of Oudh, causing anti-British feeling because there was no real reason for annexing it – apart from British greed. Now the low ratio of English to native troops is encouraging Indian nationalists to talk of taking fort William at Barrackpur while we sleep and firing telegraph house to prevent our communications.

"Frankly, I think the sepoys are dupes of those who want to rise up against the British."

"What do they have against us British?" asked William - it was more complicated than he had first thought. His friend then pointed out numerous colonial insensitivities to cast differences, like making them share the same facilities:

"We have also forbidden by law the admittedly barbarous practice of widows burning themselves on their husband's funeral pyres, as well as permitted second marriage. These may be good for women, but women are not important in India. We have also allowed sons who have changed religion to inherit, which means Christians might get father's property.

"And since 1856, new recruits in all battalions have to serve abroad, which is against the Hindu practice of not allowing casts and foreigners to mix, making them unfaithful outlaws of their own religion."

William could now see how Indian culture was being threatened and he began to question English superiority, though not in the least questioning its right to colonize.

As if to answer his doubts, his friend continued,

"In India we talk of Christian superiority and treat Indians as 'niggers', whereas in the last century we respected and integrated with them in marriage. Today, with missionaries and wives coming out from England, there is separation and condescension: English ladies don't want to mix with natives, or get to know about India. One told me she had seen nothing of the people since coming to India and didn't want to – 'the less one knows about them, the better,' she told me. Her husband also said he didn't want any beastly niggers with us!'"

"Really!" Said "William, and what do you think?"

"Well, we English who have been there a long time are different – we respect and mix with Indians, but now our science and Christianity make us 'superior' to the Asiatic, whom we call dark-skinned heathens that worship idols and evil spirits. One lady told me there is something very oppressive being surrounded by heathens, Mohammedan darkness and idol worship."

"What does the average soldier think?" asked William.

"The average British soldier only wants to get drunk and mix with prostitutes. And the average English capitalist uses whips to get through an Indian crowd, appalled that they want to be equal with us.

"Soldiers who lived here thirty years ago would scarcely credit the changes: the English are now supercilious, arrogant and contemptuous of the whole lot of them.

"Missionaries want to convert India, calling Christian religion sublime; theirs licentious and cruel. They want to free Indians from Hinduism and Mohammedanism and naturally, Indians don't like being preached at by superior foreign missionaries, when their religion is much older. They are also suspicious of our modern trains and telegraph, and our so-called 'rationalism'. After all, reason has nothing to do with belief.

"We British have invaded Afghanistan, Sind and Sikhs in the Punjab; we have annexed Jhansi - not to mention treating Nana Sahib badly by depriving him of his inheritance in Oudh. We took real power from local rulers and though we allow local practices and customs, we have used them for our own dirty work, while denying them real authority. We steal Indian raw materials and despise their culture with our dry utilitarian logic, Christian ideology and condescending evangelism.

"We have made an enemy of Nana Sahib by annexing friendly Oudh – the English governor, Lord Dalhousie, has annexed seven states, like Jhansi, in seven years with his *Doctrine of Lapse* (of ownership) which is as good as stealing land from the owners of India by using various excuses, like "inefficiency", incompetence or corruption.

The king in Delhi has already had his face moved from coinage and Nana Sahib now lives stateless, near Cawnpore. Few can understand why a harmless prince, always faithful to the British, should be so cast aside. He was not cruel to his subjects, only indulgent. And the ordinary Indian soldier has lost his previous special legal rights of connection with Britain.

"The English have also created a class of persons Indian in colour, but culturally British, who look down on their own Indian manners and culture. Meanwhile, the English have withdrawn to a life of their own – superior and exploitative, especially now their own women have arrived from England. We have taken over their land and the Indians, I am sure, will rebel.

"And soldiers who have been here thirty years who do not believe this will happen are living in the past."

"You mean the officers in Dum-Dum and Meerut and other places have misjudged the situation?"

"Yes, and the British Government has closed its eyes to the possibility of an extended plot."

Having been disappointed in action in the Crimea, William wanted to volunteer because, like English racist attitudes of the time, he thought Britain was bringing civilisation to the heathen Indian. Understandably for his time, he did not see English colonialism as a bad thing. All he could think about were the increasing massacres of European civilians, including women and children, which hardened him in his one-sided views.

Queen Victoria, who felt most Indian princes were on the side of the British, allowed the English to think it was a small body of malcontents causing the problem, rather than cruel imperialism. However, the Press soon realized the facts did not bear out the simple military mutiny theory: with murders of Europeans, it now seemed mysteriously and barbaric, propagated by fanatical religious devotees, in line with missionary accounts about India departing from the laws of god in its idolatry, pomp and luxury. The Press also suspected Russia was inflaming the minds of superstitious sepoys after the Crimean war, after, British incompetence there.

It suited William and the British to think doubts about British colonialism were groundless rooted in Indian irrationality, rather than deliberately offending religious sensibilities. And though it was true Indians feared Christianity, CPK missionaries, like Leupolt in Varanasi, denied they were hated and preferred to see the Mutiny as a battle between heathen darkness and Christian light, illustrated by a heavily-pregnant English women who had had her throat slit on her verandah, her baby cut out and laid on her breast. Others were attacked in coaches, as rebels shot every European they met.

Some English saw the Mutiny as God's punishment for lazy colonial ways in an irrational attempt to preserve a decaying Indian past. Others saw it as a Muslim plot, in which the English would save the Hindu population, though this did not explain Hindu anti-British behaviour, or **their** murder of civilians.

If William went out to fight, what would be its purpose: preserving the Empire and taking revenge on cruel native murders without examining the injustices that caused then in the first place? He thought magnanimity towards the Indian was called for and disagreed with General Neill's degraded "justice" - killing all in brutal reprisals; after all, the British had to live with the Indians in future and must accept some blame for the present situation.

William soon discovered humanitarian sentiments met with ridicule in England in April, 1857, after news began to filter through of brutal murders of British women and children all over India, especially in Cawnpore and Lucknow. And June revealed a darker side to the English racist character in its punishment of natives without guilt. William could understand heightened emotions of British soldiers seeking revenge for murdered women and children, but felt guilty about British hypocrisy. His desire for action outweighed his decided judgements, for he was itching to go to India to find the action he had missed out on in the Crimea.

He was encouraged in England by "superior" church sermons against Hindus and Muslims and the growing separation of Indian and English culture, which brought British indignation to boiling point, so that ordinary British soldiers were now mentally prepared to burn every village and hang every villager, guilty or not and blow mutineers from guns.

Returning English soldiers told William they had been amazed at the resignation of the natives, who did not struggle on the scaffold, but bore death with resignation and stoicism, smiling nonchalantly as they were hanged, as if careless of their lives.

British soldiers now became indifferent and saw the Indians as fiendish "niggers" deserving no mercy. Embarrassingly, William met returning soldiers who wanted remorselessly to annihilate the whole Indian population.

He listened to an English sermon that did not mention what cruelty his own countrymen were imposing and after spending seventeen months in Ireland, William's regiment was posted to Bombay in October 1857. A telegram informed him he was "to proceed to Liverpool immediately, *en route* for Canterbury" and he embarked on the 25 July with the transports *Blenheim* and *Monarch*, along with 28 officers, 47 sergeants and 635 other ranks to help put down the Mutiny.

As in the Crimea, the worst had already happened and he was destined to take part only in mopping up operations around the now-notorious cities of Cawnpore and Lucknow – but with much cruelty.

William - now a confident twenty-two-year-old with military experience, if not actual fighting - did not mourn too much his separation from family as he arrived at Gravesend for his boat, the *General Hewitt*. Though mainly lancers, there were also civilians on board, including wives. He took in the bustle and disorder, but passing the Needles and the coast of Hampshire, William began to feel solitary, as he had done on his trip to the Crimea, even though a spirit of adventure began steadily to pulsate.

There were then two options for Calcutta: round the Cape, or via Egypt - either way, long and perilous. The *Birkenhead* had been lost in 1852 when it hit a rock and many solders lost. William hoped he was going to Alexandria with a boat trip down the Nile, a journey of 130 miles, with a stay in Cairo.

"Much better," said his friend, "to go like Frederick Roberts, from Southampton to Alexandria and board a Nile boat for Cairo. His journey had taken seven hours, plus a ten-mile hike to see the pyramids."

On board, William got into conversation with an experienced cockney solider who had originally gone via South Africa, which William discovered was to be his own route:

"It'd bloody hot out there. Cape horn takes one-hundred-and-twenty-one days – seventeen weeks - stormy and dangerous, but better now with the new paddle steamers. They weigh 7000 tons. There are few vacancies for wives and children, so most couples suffer years of separation and hardship. Some women pretend to be men in order to get on board.

"You will be as close together with your fellow soldiers as fingers on one hand, with much talking and swearing – not to mention drinking to excess, especially when crossing the line, before being ducked. You will not be allowed ashore - only officers. Your children might die of cholera, but if they do, there will be a good send off with *God Save the Queen* played by the band. After that there will be nothing to do but play cards and attend parade on the poop deck."

William was inspected for cleanliness every day, along with his hammock, and paraded without shoes or stockings to check his feet. Fortunately, he did not suffer from seasickness and was an "abstainer", though the ship's drinking water was very black and smelled vile.

While crossing the Indian Ocean, William also began to feel religious, so that the spirit of God came to him, providing great relief in future tribulations: He thought of his vicar back in Pleasley and started reading his Bible, scribbling notes in the margins and decorating its inside covers with favourite quotes, such as, "He is able to keep you from falling", so that his great-grandchildren were able to read this Bible in the late 21st century.

 He had been taught to read by his local vicar and the words of his sermon came to mind when he talked - like many Christians - of the evil Hindus' belief in caste and suttee: the burning of widows of the dead. And now there were the murders in the Cawnpore *bibighat,* on the banks of the Ganges, when the wicked Nana Sahib tricked Wheeler into surrender with promises of saving them. The mutineers were in no way to be trusted, though William could not believe they were all bad.

He shared a cabin with five other recruits, and they exchanged histories. His swinging cot - only fourteen inches wide - was most comfortable, though sleep did not come easily because they were all so excited at what lay ahead.

He enjoyed watching 100 skipjacks (tuna) leaping out of the water, making him laugh, shout and point like a child. He caught a rash called "prickly heat" when they neared the Equator, where he was shaved by "Neptune", along with the rest of the passengers crossing for the first time. The crew were also shaved and ducked, laughing while officers threw water over each other from buckets.

In the evening he joined the dancing and singing, drinking a little grog to the seamen's chant of:

We'll lather away

And shave away so fine

We always have a shaving day

Whenever we cross the line.

There's nothing half so sweet in life

As crossing of the line,

followed by *Rule Britannia*.

Meanwhile, his fellow soldiers amused themselves shooting at albatross's, floating majestically round the boat and blithely ignoring the guns. Later, the men gambled with pitch and toss, boxed or played chess and backgammon, continuing into the evening. Then there was an eclipse of the moon, followed by a gale that split the main sale and blew the others to pieces, so that the boat was now tossed around like a cork.

Another ship, heading back to England drew up alongside, reminding William of his family back in Pleasley Vale and making him sad for a while, before once more looking ahead to his own exciting future, so that he did not once think of his father and mother.

Next, his ship was becalmed - far worse than the gale – a miserable heavy swell without a ripple on the sea, so that the ship stopped moving forward and her timbers groaning as if in pain. A boat was lowered and some went out shooting, returning with an albatross (nine foot from wing to wing when outstretched), a Cape hen, sea swallow and other birds. He saw a whale, but it did not come so near as to threaten. Then a school of twenty or thirty approached, spouting and playing and the ship's seamen hit a big one with a Congreve weapon and it sank, in a few seconds exploding.

In the next calm, there was a great slaughter of sea game and the ship's cruel terrier seized a large, fierce blackbird with broken wing, eventually getting it by the throat and receiving several scratches which drew blood. And when the ship's company caught a shark and opened it, there were twenty-four young ones inside.

Despite these distractions, William soon began to yearn for the end of his voyage, wondering how he would cope with India's "vertical" sun and its language. Meanwhile, one of his regiment fell overboard and was lost because it was not noticed till next day. He would never see India, which made William ponder the vagaries of fate and wonder if he would ever see home again.

A regimental band played *God Save the Queen* to a passing vessel and he heard three cheers. Then, yet more calm:

Day after day, day after day

We stuck nor breath not motion

As idle as a painted ship

Upon a painted ocean

As Bombay neared, William began to think more about the Mutiny, beginning as a small cloud of dissatisfaction, no bigger than a man's hand, but might now grow to threaten the ruin of the Raj. And all because Indian sepoys had been led to believe their cartridges were smeared with pig or cow's wax, against their Hindu and Muslim religious beliefs.

William thought principles very strange things when based on illogical thinking. Or were they being manipulated by darker nationalist forces? But then, British policy was all based on its inalienable right to India, rather than the facts.

He now began to think the spontaneity of the outbreaks all over the north of India must have other, deeper causes: fear of missionary propaganda, British theft of land from local rulers, rules and regulations stemming from current Utilitarian principles and anti-Indian culture – maybe there was even a coordinated Indian conspiracy. And finally, British separation from Indian customs and imposition of Western ways, like the railway, steamship and new communications. Britain thought modernity was always right, but was it appropriate in India?

William also noted how new English officers often hated and maltreated Indians: "black man" were despised as "horrible nigger sepoys", whereas the previous generation of British soldiers had liked and married Indian. Now segregation, encouraged by superior Christian missionaries, looked down on Hindus and Muslims, while the increasing presence of British wives made socialization difficult.

Britain's recent defeat in Afghanistan and poor performance in the Crimea had been well-noted by nationalistic Indians. And, a Hindu now being ordered to cross the water to fight in Persia, China or Burma was unthinkable because of religious and inevitable caste violations, even though new Indian soldiers had to take an oath that they would travel.

Then, there was the numerical fact that Indians made up the majority of the British army in India by ten to one, which only slowly began to reverse with new arrivals from Britain, of which William was one – so the British would be in a minority if it came to a future fight.

In Oudh, many Bengal Army sepoys were from high-caste and landowning communities, making for increasing unrest, as their privileges and customary allowances were now withdrawn. And with this uncertainty, their status both as soldiers and citizens was under threat.

INDIA

After a four-month voyage, at the end of November, William reached Calcutta, where he was informed his regiment was to go Allahabad with the utmost speed to join Hope Grant's Cavalry Division in Sir Colin Campbell's force - a 500-mile journey, 400 miles of which entailed marching across India with newly-issued horses.

Most of the new men, like William, aged only twenty-two, had never been out of Britain, let alone seen service in the East. He was to be employed, during this latter stage of the Mutiny, in mopping-up operations and in March 1858 took part in the siege of Lucknow, centre of rebel operations, from his new base in Cawnpore.

At the start of the Mutiny, the rebels had seized Lucknow, besieged the British and cooped them up in the Residency. With a small force, Havelock had fought his way through to the beleaguered garrison, reaching them just in time, but both the beleaguered and the relievers then had to endure a second siege. In the autumn of 1857, Sir Colin Campbell, with a second relief column, managed to raise the siege, but did not have sufficient strength to capture the town. He therefore retired with what remained of the garrison and its imprisoned Europeans. Now in February 1858 he was assembling a force of 20,000 men to march on Lucknow, held by 130,000 mutineers.

On the 6th March, William was among two squadrons of Bays under the command of Major Percy Smith who made a spirited charge against the sepoys, suffering nine casualties. His letter to family in Pleasley described it:

About 10am we came on bodies of enemy cavalry and infantry and the Bays were ordered to charge and pursue. Major Smith was leading. We did not stop for three miles, pursuing and cutting up the Pandies right up to Lucknow and across the river. However, we lost our best officer, shot dead within five yards of myself, with some 15 men. Poor Major Smith! He fell without a groan. I and four of our troop tried to bring his body off, but their cavalry numbers made it impossible.

The remaining corporal of my Troop, whose horse would not let him get up, was cut to ribbons! I returned without a scratch, though my charger got a nasty sabre wound on his off-foreleg, which will prevent my riding him for some time. We captured an elephant, and killed between sixty and seventy mutineers.

On the 16 March we finally cleared the mutineers from Lucknow, but 20,000 sepoys managed to escape to fight another day. Sir Colin Campbell despatched two cavalry brigades to chase the rebels, but their cavalry scattered all over the countryside and we had little success. With the capture of Lucknow, operations were now concerned with the pacification of the countryside.

But by the middle of May the heat was so bad that hardened troops were dying in scores. Troops usually executed captured prisoners, armed or not. William Hodson, who led an irregular cavalry unit, was killed during the capture of the Begum Kothi on 11 March.

William became now puzzled over the question of whether the "Mutiny" was an Indian national war of independence - the Indians were later to call it the First War of Independence, though it was confined mainly to the north round Oudh and Bengal.

He continued to read newspapers from home about the Meerut, Cawnpore and Lucknow massacres and the "terrible" Nana Sahib. The behaviour of the British towards Indian freedom – their taking of land and the imposition of the cartridge did not concern him too much and as an Englishman, for he was taken with the usual feelings of colonial superiority, angry at the treatment of women in the many massacres, especially at Cawnpore, where he was now stationed – the scene of the terrible events earlier in 1857.

A short, spare, grey-haired man of sixty-seven - Wheeler had spent nearly all his life in India. He loved the country and his sepoys, whose language he spoke as well as they themselves. He had married an Indian woman and refused to believe there would be any serious trouble with the four native Cawnpore regiments, though they outnumbered the British ten to one. His commanding officers had also expressed complete trust in the staunchness of their men and did not think they would turn on the Europeans.

But he had reckoned without the English treatment of Nana Sahib, adopted son of Dhondu Pant, who had refused an inheritance and pension when his father was deposed by the British. He therefore, understandably bore a deep grudge and became rebel leader. His chief advisor had helpfully noted the deplorable condition of the British army in the Crimea.

Wheeler first moved the women and children into the barrack entrenchment, which was poorly defended, with only a four-foot wall. Officers were withdrawn from sleeping alongside their Indian men because of the coming mutiny, and Wheeler's initial optimism that the sepoys would leave to make for Delhi were disappointed because Nana Sahib, by way of personal revenge, wanted to annihilate the British in Cawnpore. He arrived on June 6th 1855 under two banners – Mohammed and the Hanuman Monkey god, representing the two religions, and declared himself Peshwa (hereditary leader). Tantia Topi was his able commander.

His attack on the settlement killed three-hundred-and-thirty men, women and children. Many of his men were on edible cannabis or *bhang* - "the devil's wind". In the British settlement, the dead were thrown down the sixty-foot well to avoid disease and a volunteer to fetch water would typically last only one week before being shelled (usually people crept there in the dead of night to avoid death). It was so hot (128-130 degrees Fahrenheit) that guns went off by themselves.

Nana Sahib cut off the noses and ears of captured Europeans, before killing them and murdered a boatload of women and children coming up the Ganges. By 26th June, the situation had become desperate for the British.

Then, a white women came bearing a note from Sahib offering safe passage to Allabad, but all the men were murdered in the water when they got into the boats, including Wheeler and his elder daughter. One-hundred-and-twenty-five women were pulled out of the water.

William had read of Nana Sahib's Cawnpore bibighar Massacre while in England. How General Havelock had decided to attack on the flank – a severe march where the sun struck with force so that at every step a man fell down from the ranks, calling for water. The Highlanders were ordered to charge, other soldiers vying with Havelock for the honour. The rebel line was broken, but Sahib escaped, along with thousands who feared British retribution.

When General Neil arrived in July 1857, he took revenge on all Indians for their slaughter of women in the House of the Ladies. William later visited the *bibighar* in November and saw ladies' and children's clothes, strewn about on a floor, still clotted with blood: where bodies had been dragged, they had left a bloody trail on trees and ground. Soldiers picked up strands of hair to reinforce their hysterical hatred of the Indian, from sights they would never forget.

Four months later William was stationed in Cawnpore (after arriving in India on November 17th). He pondered the ruthless murders as an unspeakable crime, for women were then regarded in England as "angels of the hearth"; but he could not understand why Neill had been so indiscriminately brutal in reprisals, forcing Indians to kneel down and lick up blood before their often unfair executions.

And castes were broken by forcing pork and beef down the throats of suspected rebels. Neill's justification was "I will hold my own, with the blessing help of God – I cannot help seeing that his finger is in all this." So much for his understanding of the nature of his Christian god. These punishments continued for months.

On arrival in Cawnpore, William's regiment marched through the streets to the bibighar to see the scene of the terrible massacre, for themselves: children's socks, shoes and dresses covered in fading blood and the brains of the innocent, along with large quantities of hair. He did not to pick anything up, but swore to be revenged in spades on those "black-faced curs" for their slaughter of English women and children.

"When this crisis is over," said one of his captains, "the Indian must be kept in his place. It is ridiculous to talk of mercy in the most horrible business every perpetrated in India by the niggers."

It was common now in England to talk of "dearer" and "cheaper" races, ie., the rest of the world, including Ireland, and conflict between the two, resulting in inevitable triumph of the former. Darwin's recent talk of natural selection had now made this almost "scientific". Interestingly, no passports were needed to come and live in England, despite - or perhaps because of - British feelings of superiority.

In this atmosphere, William found it difficult to be rational about his new enemy as he prepared to join in the relief of Lucknow under Sir Colin Campbell, who had arrived on 14th November, three days before William arrived.

After the appalling slaughter, his men wanted revenge for Cawnpore's "bloody women murderers" in the bibighar. The mutineers fought back like devils, so that before long, the ground was writhing with bodies, as the fighting progressed from room to room, bodies piled five-feet-high in places, the wounded unable to detach themselves from the dead. Bodies were thrown out and landed with a sickening thud on the ground below. Sixty-four men were drawn up and mercilessly bayonetted to yells of "Cawnpore"!

Soon they were ready to attack the Residency itself, which was hard work. Finally, "sir" Henry, seeing that the city still swarmed with rebels and he had had to get five-hundred women and children out, he decided the best thing for the moment was evacuation, before later clearing the rebels from Cawnpore.

William learned of the November 19th Cawnpore evacuation in Calcutta, before being posted to help. The bibighar Massacre of two-hundred-and-ten ladies had taken place in a small bungalow of the women and children who had survived Nana Sahib's previous boat massacre. But with only 1,100 Europeans and 300 Sikhs, frontal attack was suicide, so Havelock had decided to go round the left flank to the back, where he had promised young captain Currie promotion if he acquitted himself well: but one of the first shots took away nearly the whole of his lower body and he lingered for three days, drinking champagne. Gunners were not supposed to duck because it was bad form and there was competition to be the first to charge or attack.

Havelock camped two miles outside Cawnpore in the heat of an Indian sun and fought four actions against overwhelming odds. Then he came to the bibighar – thickly caked with blood, where many bodies had been thrown into a well, a ghastly tangle of naked limbs, where Indians were forced to lick up the blood in revenge for the women's murders.

British Soldiers in Cawnpore had already started drinking and taking revenge on the local population, while locals of high caste were made to lick up the blood, force fed pork and beef, before being hanged. Thousands were killed without the least pretence of a legal process.

At this point William arrived with six hundred cavalry recently arrived from England and Campbell successfully attacked Tatya Tope, though thousands of rebels escaped, despite surrounding areas being under British control.

William was among cavalry sent out to surrounding villages, looking for rebels whom his sergeant described as "Brutes deserving no mercy". The general British opinion was that sepoys could not be regarded as human beings, and should be destroyed like reptiles. William was told that no one would leave a sepoy alive, much less wounded and that they were to be hung on trees to rot. "These damned niggers are lower than the brutes" was a common opinion. William began to be affected by these sentiments, though he still could hardly believe what his young ears heard.

After exhausting cross country marches, where he was now able to fire at the rebels from a distance of one thousand yards, William now returned to camp to relax, where fellow soldiers play games, gambled and ate well. He was also able to read English papers, largely featuring the Mutiny. Attention now turned to Lucknow, where the rebels had gathered an enormous army. Fortunately, Britain's was now the largest ever been in India and the British were ruthless and rode roughshod over Indians.

In Delhi, garrisoned largely by sepoys and no British regiments, there were many massacres of Europeans - but no rape, despite what British said about savages, while praising the Gurkhas for ripping open Indians with long knives (kukree)

The final war of reprisal in 1858-9 against Ramchandra Pandenanga, or Tatya Tope, was seen as a war on barbarism by Christians for the honour of Britain. British cruelty was redoubled: hanging was too good for them: they were stripped, tied to ground and branded all over, before having their brains blown out, or a bayoneted prisoners slowly roasted over a fire, sewn into pigskins and smeared with fat. Before Karnpur, the British raped and pillaged and burned alive, enjoying "amazingly" "peppering away at niggers", or blowing them from mouths of canon, or forcing them to lick the floor of blood and trying to break their cast. Colonel James Neill killed more in Allahabad than were lost by his own side in two years of fighting.

Britain now took over India directly, with rights to revenues and rents of princes and peasant farmers. It also appropriated the role of educator, disapproving of Indian religions. Parliament abolished the East India Company and India was transferred to Victoria as Empress of India. The racist English hated the Indians, though most sepoys remained loyal!

The King of Delhi was put on trial and exiled to Rangoon; Tatya Tope was hanged in April 1859, Lord Canning became viceroy and India was modernised by busybody liberalism.

William was marching through well-cultivated countryside, with dark mango trees inhabited by scuttling, chattering monkeys, hanging by one leg, or their tail. He saw many skeletons of dead rebels with fleshless limbs and white-toothed horrid grins on ghastly skulls. When the army split in two William joined Campbell's group in the west.

He would vividly remember his first battle for the rest of his life: first, horses' heads deep in nose bags and officers handing round cigar cases and brandy flasks. Men would then eat what for many would be their last meal – carving bread and lumps of meat with pocket knives. The battle began with the enemy firing screaming shots through mango trees, tearing up ground before the soldiers. Then they chased rebels, killing one after another, finishing them off with bayonets - usually without mercy.

There were horrible scenes of sepoys stripped and branded with red hot irons on every part of their bodies, or stabbed and roasted over an open fire - even innocent villagers. English blood was up: "his skin was black, wasn't that enough?"

Lucknow was re-captured on 16th March and William observed thousands of dead bodies among the debris of war, Indians shot without question, or mercy. Then followed looting by British soldiers drunk with the desire for gold, while thousands of rebels fled across the river, leaving the finest city in India with hordes of decomposing corpses, defeated by the firepower of the British Enfield.

British "civilisation" broke when her soldiers hanged scores, leaving legs to be eaten away by pigs, and subjecting "niggers" to indiscriminate punishment, village after village. So much for English manners, supported by Christian religion, thought William.

"Superior" Christian sentiment had it that "the blessings of the Almighty had put the British on the righteous cause of justice". One English Christian hero, Robert Tucker, who refused to leave the town, died on his roof, pistol in one hand, Bible in the other, killing a dozen before succumbing himself. Religion was supposed to be about peace and friendship, but in Cawnpore, William's head now rang with the cries of revenge on Nana Sahib and the sermons of missionaries and chaplains calling for blood and appealing to the heavens for vengeance on the wicked Indian nation. One of his officers told him of "a violent demonstration after dinner about niggers and their desserts…I cannot understand any Englishman sympathising with them."

By Sept 23rd just sixteen miles from Lucknow, William approached a two-mile wall of 10,000 sepoy rebels. Delhi had fallen to the British by now, to loud cheering. In a battle on 22nd and 23rd November, William saw savage fighting and severe reprisals on sepoy rebels – which made him question his Christian beliefs.

***

Next, William joined the struggle in Jhansi, annexed by Lord Dalhousie under his infamous doctrine of Lapse against the famous Queen Rani, aided by the infamous Tatia Tope. During 1858, William's regiment marched 2,028 miles and camped three hundred times, as he joined the fighting columns marching through Raputana in pursuit of the notoriously successful rebel leader Tatya Tope (eventually defeated by Sir Colin Campbell on December 6, 1857). Finally, the Rani of Jhansi, who led her troops on horseback dressed as a man, was shot and killed by one of William's own regiment.

Her kingdom had been treated unfairly under Dalhousie's Doctrine of Lapse and she was not initially a rebel, even after her appeal against confiscation was rejected in London, but she finally decided to fight what she saw as British injustice. William had been told that she was still beautiful, if a little stout, and a brave soldier. She was civil, polite and clever and the English had trusted her to protect them in Jhansi.

However, on 8th June 57, they were massacred and the rebels left next day. She was sorry, but threatened by the rebels with blowing up her palace, she could not ensure the safety of foreigners. The English were skeptical of her protests of innocence and ignored her appeals for help, so she turned to the rebels to defend Jhansi, until the British army under Hugh Rose turned up in March 1858, intent on revenge. William was among the soldiers laying siege

It was relentlessly hot with blasts of wind, so that the gunners wrapped wet towels round their heads and

William looked for shade outside the walls while awaiting a breach. Strange cheering from inside revealed that Tatia Tope had turned up, so that William and the English were now sidetracked with an attack by a second army of 20,000 Indian mutineers.

He was told to spare no-one over sixteen – except women of course - and five thousand were soon killed. Most of the rebels fled to join Tati Tope and the Rani.

On 6th after an exhausting fourteen mile May walk, they came on the rebels at Kunch, exhausted with heat and thirsty. William watched as his fellow soldiers fall dead from heat stroke, collapsing, sobbing and laughing hysterically as they cried deliriously for water. He attempted pursuit but his horse was knocked out.

They lost seven men from sunstroke and four officers were not expected to live. It was 115 degrees in their tents and William's sword was so hot he could hardly handle it. Everyone begged for water. At Kalpi, one of the strongest forts in India, on 22nd May, the rebels swore on the sacred waters of the Jumna to defeat the Feringhis, or die.

On Victoria's birthday, the British flag was unfurled over the Indian fort. The rebels near Gwalior did not look as if they could do another battle. But next day, they were joined by other princes and Rose had to abandon thoughts of taking leave.

Next day, the Rani of Jhansi, dressed as a man, reins in her mouth, using her sword with both hands, was struck and killed - shot in the back by an 8th Hussar trooper and when she turned to fire back she was run through with a sword. William witnessed this, along with eighty-four men incapacitated by sun stroke. In hot pursuit of mutineers he went to the edge of a forest and saw a British shell "explode" an Indian who suddenly appeared out of a wood and was blown him to pieces."

For eight months, Tatya Tope had eluded capture but by October the rebellion was dying out and Tope was betrayed, captured and hanged in April 1859 and Nana Sahib disappeared into Nepal. The old king of Delhi was put on trial in a military court for allowing himself to be crowned king of India – a sorry figure who was transported to Rangoon, where his descendants still live today.

This was a British war of no pity, with locals hanged on the least excuse just for being Indian so that trees swung with thousands, a common occurrence William would never forget. His unit joined in operations to clear the state of Oude – ruthlessly carried out with no quarter given.

Finally, in July 1859 his regiment returned to Lucknow at the end of the hot season, when the weather became very sultry and soldiers waited anxiously for the rainy season, as normal regimental life now resumed. During the more clement cold season on 22ⁿᵈ November William got a good conduct badge with a 1d a day pay rise and was promoted to corporal on 1ˢᵗ Feb 1860.

In 1862, his regiment moved to Benares Barracks, one of the hottest stations in India, so he was glad of the start of the Cold season. He was sad to learn that his father in Pleasley, Mansfield, had died at the ripe old age of sixty-three. During the war he had heard nothing from home because he had been constantly on the move, but now he wrote his condolences to mother and explained why he could not yet go home. He got a second good conduct badge and pay increase on 9ᵗʰ January 1863, before volunteering for the unattached list on 13ᵗʰ October 1863.

He was now transferred to the staff, where he worked for General Lord Roberts, after twelve months becoming a staff sergeant. While in barracks forty kilometres from Varanasi, he often visited Leupolt's Mission for Christian fellowship, where his life was to change forever, because he met and married Amelia (15 years old, a child during the Mutiny of which she remembered nothing, for she was sent to the hills to avoid the fighting zones).[7]

---

[7] Here, for want of hard evidence, my History has to submit to fiction because, though the writer has been told by family that William was introduced to "a begum" while visiting her house with Lord Roberts, this has been questioned by academic experts because it would have been unthinkable for a man of lower ranks to be introduced just after the Mutiny. It is therefore probably a family myth to lend respectability to the "distasteful" idea of an Englishman marrying an Indian foreigner – especially if she turned out to be an orphan, which this writer has reason

Here, we must seek the assistance of CB Leupolt, who wrote two volumes of memoirs about his time setting up and officiating over the Benares SPCK Mission, before William and Amelia met and married there. William himself was posted just outside at Fort Chunar, forty-five km from central Varansi, where Leupolt had another church mission.

Benares was flat, fertile and one of the hottest stations, with plenty of snakes and troublesome mosquitos, (though fortunately, they nearly disappeared during the "cold" and very hot seasons). Its finest view was from the southern side of the river Ganges, looking over numerous ghauts, or steps, down to the river. It had no rice fields, but there were many small snakes - the hooded *cobra capella* - being most dangerous.

William discovered the sun was so hot that people slept outdoors, though they also superstitiously feared the effects of moon beams almost as much as snakes and took precautions to keep out of their rays, for fear of the "damaging" their human constitution.

After airless and exhausting sun, William welcomed the rainy season of July, beginning with noisy thunderstorms: the relief was welcome and his

---

to believe. A distant relative of one of William's sons tells me, "My understanding is that 'Padam' can be an Indian surname. 'Gurpreet Padam' or 'Singh Padam' are not particularly unusual, for example, among Sikhs."

energy revived. Thousands of frogs then made so much noise that he could not sleep. Every tank and pool was filled with small fish, and it rained for days, so that thousands of white ants took wing and invaded homes.

Many houses collapsed during the rain and lives were lost in the constant roar of thunder and vivid lightning. Leupolt liked to quote the Psalm: the "voice of thunder was in the heaven" and "lightning lightened the world"..."as the earth trembled and shook."

His Christian god was hands-on, behind everything, so he often got into trouble debating publically with other religions over whether He was behind sin, since he had first created it, along with Adam. Leupolt enjoyed the cut and thrust of discussion because of his Western Christian "superiority", whose colonisation permitted it to think it would easily convert the "heathen".

William thought colourful India very beautiful and came to enjoy the extremes of temperature. He loved to walk near the huge Arungzebe Muslim church, built by Arunth along the bank of the Ganges, comparing it favourably with his native Pleasley. It was built on the ruins of a Hindu temple, tall and majestic, with very high minarets at its grand entrance and grand views across the Ganges.

The German, Leupolt - who had been in India since 1832, apart from two years break in England - had witnessed the Mutiny and William got to know him through attending the church Mission, interested in his views on the recent Mutiny, as well as his beautiful Amelia Padam.

Strangely, in view of its central position, Benares had escaped the worst of Mutiny violence. Wisely, Leupolt had foreseen the conflict as early as the 1840's because of what he called India's "pernicious system of education which, he thought had nourished vipers at home". He had warned that education in the *Koran* and the *Shasters* - excluding the Bible - and forbidding Christian converts in the ranks of the native army would not secure loyal native subjects and that one day the British would pay the political penalty.

William began attending Leupolt's church services, welcoming the opportunity to meet fellow English Christians. He discovered Leupolt took every opportunity to talk to and convert those whom he was fond of calling "the heathen" - especially Muslims, so that William himself began to take on some of the German's superior Christian prejudices towards Muslims and Hindus – views that were common in England before the Mutiny, where Leupolt had trained with the SPCK (Society for the Promotion of Christian Knowledge).

Leupolt's prejudices saw Indian religions as pictures of sin – the Muslims for their profligacy, the Hindus for their disregard of truth. "In other respects," he sourly noted, "they resemble each other," drawing a dark picture of both religions with little to redeem them, except for Hindu contentment in no thought for the morrow and lack of unifying patriotism, which Leupolt thought would not make them anti-British. Unlike the Muslims, who told Leupolt, "if you were not our rulers we would soon silence your preaching, not with argument, but with the sword."

Leupolt thought it wrong not to educate and expand Indian minds with Western knowledge, for it left the heart empty and void, minus heavenly wisdom, with the desire to destroy all the English in their country: "God has given you India; beware how you use your power, for he can take it away from you."

He thought the Hindus obsessed with class differences:

"If I can ride in a conveyance, I do not ride on horseback; if I can stand, I do not go in a conveyance; if I can sit, I do not stand; and if I can lie, I do not sit."

And Leupolt was particularly exercised by the life of Hindu women - miserable, never free and unkindly treated. The woman's chosen religious role was to sweep the house, cook and please her husband in her adornment. Finally, she would ascend the funeral pyre to be burned with her dead husband in agony and despair. In 1839, when Runjeet Sing died, fifteen of his wives and concubines were burned. Though the practise was now ended, the wife was still strictly prohibited from re-marrying, must now have no more than one coarse meal a day and sleep on the ground.[8]

William was interested to learn from Leupolt that the Mutiny in Benares had had no European troops, nor disaffected native soldiers, though it had a population of potentially "bigoted" Hindus and Mohammedans and, of course was the holy capital of Brahminism. And yet the English Commissioner had shown no fear, riding unharmed about the city with his daughter. The conflict had been confined only to the troops opposed by the vicious General Neil, while the city itself remained perfectly calm and the country people apathetic.

This was amazing, in view of Benares position on the Ganges between Delhi, Cawnpore and Calcutta, where there had been widespread murder of Europeans and burning of homes. Benares had been responsible for providing food to troops moving up the river, handling scarcity so well that prices did not rice.

If Leupolt had known what "god-fearing" General Neil had been doing in Allahabad, he might have amended his story, for the general did not believe in Christian tenderness in India – prompt execution of all suspected rebels was his solution. There, European volunteers and Sikhs had descended on the town burning and slaughtering everyone in sight

---

[8] In 2018, a quarter of all female suicides are Indian

after laughable "trials". William was told that "every day, a dozen niggers were hanged from branches of signposts all over town."

In Cawnpore, Neil had been savage in ferocious treatment murderers of women and children in the "house of the ladies". Many English told William how they could not understand how anyone could sympathise with "niggers". And as soon as Neil reached Benares, he had insisted on disarming of the Indian 37th, opening fire on the Sepoys and hanging scores, including boys.

During the Mutiny, Leupolt had remained in the city's Church compound, where native Anglicised Christians were distrusted by the rebels. Since the mutiny, many had joined the police who, in Leupolt's jaundiced Christian opinion, "had a higher standard of honesty, truth and duty than natives". He believed that the only thing that would benefit natives was "a good vernacular Bible education for the masses."

His mission provided cheap education for the church missionary society. And the commissioner told William, "what can indeed be reasonably expected from heathen teachers, many old and stupid, who had never had any training for their work?"

Leupolt was highly praised all round, despite his view of native religions - the common British view at a time when Indians were considered no higher than ignorant and untrustworthy "niggers". Despite famous Indian native tolerance for all religions –

Buddhism, Islam and Hinduism - his arrogantly-superior mission aimed to convert the whole of the native population from their own time-honoured religions, though he did not expect quick results in getting rid of India's idols – they had been around too long. However, aided by the Holy Spirit, he expected, finally, to rid India of its numerous idolatrous practices, like the Romans in their empire and bring people up in knowledge of the "true god", through his son, Jesus.

William soon learned about British condescension towards other religions and for the most part agreed, having seen sepoys murdering women and children. On the other hand, the British had been without pity and often killed thousands of blameless civilians in revenge. He was therefore very interested to know why there had been no civilian killings in Benares and whether it had anything to do with the different way the British had treated foreigners there.

Yet Leupolt's attitude to Hindus and Muslims appeared condescending and superior, the normal European attitude towards Hindoostan – "place of the blacks". But Indians also thought the British foolish, with their "Reason", Utilitarianism, steam engines, paper mills and balloons – and, worst of all, their religion based on belief in an old paper book - The *Bible* – which said the world was only 6,000 years old – how foolish: one of the Indian Rajahs had ruled for 10,000 years!

AMELIA

Leupolt's Christian crusade in the holy Hindu city where Shiva was said to have reigned was viewed by many as foolishly-arrogant. Amelia, one of his successful converts - though a homeless orphan could not be considered much of a Hindu threat and probably had had little choice but to become a Christian, since the Mission provided her with food, so that conversion had probably been the price of her food and education.

Though the Uprising altered relations between the British and Indians, the reality of life wasn't always as black and white as it might have seemed through the lens of separatist Mutiny history. Intermarriage between white British and Indians might not now be encouraged, as today's scholars now insist, but that didn't mean it didn't happen, especially when facilitated by circumstances like William's at Leupolt' church.

Amelia had no obvious European ancestry: Eurasian might have been a possibility - her parents might have been Hindus converted to Christianity who left Amelia an orphan – or placed her at the Mission because they could not afford to bring her up as a Christian in a volatile situation.

When William Lacey met fifteen-year-old Amelia in the church congregation, the army authorities would not have had a problem with him marrying a

Chistian-ised Indian orphan - even after the 1857 rebellion - if she was vouched for by Leupolt. Probably her new religion was of greater importance than her ethnicity.

William's growing attraction to this slender, attractive young Indian led him to attend Leupolt's services regularly and he became increasingly infatuated with her *petite* hands and fingers, amazingly long and slender. She was not tall, but her slim figure was attractively demure. The sexual spell was cast and he could no longer take his eyes off her: the result was inevitable.

One day, when she left the service directly in front of him, Leupolt introduced them:

"Amelia, this is William Lacey, whom we have to thank for saving us from the Sepoy rebels."

She smiled, said hello and added, "I hope he is not also responsible for the many British injustices done to our people." Demure, but not without sharp opinions, noticed William - rather like his own English mother.

Leupolt's sermon, as usual, had decried native Indian idolatory, praised the superiority of his own religion and the inadequacy of the native to measure up to it:

"God has given India all that man can desire, but the natives are not thankful for those gifts – *every prospect pleases, and only man is vile...the heathen in his blindness bows down to wood and stone.*"

At first, Amelia had found these superior British sentiments towards her own people condescendingly mean, but as she approached Christian conversion, she began to notice – his religious opinions notwithstanding - Leupolt's gentler character. He was a good man, kind and caring - and she began to take to him, at last being converted by his combination of English colonial materialism, though she could not agree with all his opinions.

William noticed, apart from her bodily attraction (she was short, slender and well-proportioned), that Amelia was also blessed with outstanding gentleness: a listener rather than a talker and very practical, her dark brown eyes drawing William in with tenderness and empathy. But he also began to respect her strong political opinions and compare them – often unfavourably - with his own English views, for example, her scorn for English imperialism.

He could also see his own British illogicality in insisting there was one god, with a capital "G", when other religions differed and argued for their own one god. This insistence meant that Christianity was either right or totally wrong, with no middle position. Better to have compromised on god and shared his qualities so that all could share a bit of truth – god with a small "g" that might be shared.

Later, Leupolt told William that Amelia's parents had been Hindus who had died in an outbreak of disease, after which she had converted to Christianity at his

Mission School, where she had also learned excellent English.

William decided he wanted to get to know this attractive native girl and took every opportunity to discuss India and his own part in the rights and wrongs of British colonialism. In particular, he was interested in what the Indians – and by implication Amelia - thought of him.

"Why did the Indians hate us so much they believed we would deliberately give them greased cartridges, causing this terrible mutiny and the killing of men, women and children?"

"These were only an excuse: the truth is that England has stolen our country and Dalhousie robbed our kings of their lands with his silly *Doctrine of Lapse*, which was merely an excuse. You stole India and deprived our King of Delhi of his rights, so that he is now an exile. You have arrogantly imposed Christianity where Hindus and Muslims have long learned to live tolerantly in peace – so naturally, they resent it.

"Also, you disbanded our sepoy regiments and took away their rights. And as for Nana Sahib, the murderer of women and children at Cawnpore, he had just cause for hating you: losing his pension turned him against the British – the reason why his butchers massacred the men women and children in Cawnpore, though, of course, I cannot condone this."

William once more raised his British feelings of disgust at the Bibighat and Lady's House murders in Cawnpore, which had increased the British hatred of the Indian. Also the needless killing of men women and children in most Indian cities where mutinies had taken place. Indeed, this had first attracted him to the idea of fighting – to right wrongs – because he was too young to realise that he was simply part of the British colonial usurpation of India, soon to be *the jewel in the British crown*. Youthfully, he like to think he was not to blame for thinking what most English thought at the time.

"But," said Amelia, "you made things worse with your murderous reprisals and thousands of roadside gibbets for innocent Indians. For sheer barbarity our massacre of innocents was rivalled and surpassed by disgusting British reprisals. And you are supposed to be a civilised country!"

William had to admit that this had been a war without pity and blushed bright red beneath his red uniform and sunburn.

"I saw it myself at Cawnpore and Lucknow," he said quietly, "and I wonder if we can ever forgive one another. Lucknow was a horrible siege lasting five months - a holy place of British Imperialism, but animal revenge for Cawnpore. I was there in 1858 and was ashamed of my country. I am also ashamed to say that I also saw the killing of Queen Lakshima in Jhansi by one of our regiment, the 8th Hussars."

William began to consider how he might finally bridge the diminishing gap between his growing attraction for Amelia and cruel British colonial greed. In true love there could be no colonising impulse, though the male/female sexist divide was strong in India.

Amelia continued,

"Since the end of the Mutiny, the proportion of British to Indian troops has been drastically increased in your favour by three to one. Expansion of rail and telegraph have improved your communications. If anything, one day, we Indians will hate you even more for your vicious greed."

"But," said William, "Victoria has now forbidden British interference in Indian religious traditions. And even Bentham's Utilitarianism is now seen as inappropriate for India."

"But," replied Amelia, "our Landowners are now respectful, faithful allies of our British rulers and Victoria Queen is Empress of India. We now shamelessly mirror your system of honours and hierarchy!

"Let us face it, Britain's political and religious superiority has won the day. You take us to be heathen idiot 'nincompoops' who dislike modern science and prefer superstition. But one day soon we Indians will demand our independence, mark my words, if not this century, then next.

"Yu have only got to look at Leupolt's condescending attitude to Hindus in this Holy City of Benares, arrogant caring man that he may be. The British have been here since 1776 - the place where Shiva is supposed to have reigned: the formless, limitless, transcendent and unchanging absolute and primal soul of the universe, the Supreme Being the preserver, protector.

"How can England hope to compare: Benares is the centre of the earth, 80,000 steps nearer heaven than anywhere else in this world. Ten miles around is holy ground, and whoever dies here will go to Heaven, though he be the greatest sinner in the world. And yet your arrogant empire looks down on us!"

"Yes, said William, "People don't mind being wicked here because they are told they will go to heaven. They come here to die and there are many pilgrims to the sacred spot where Shiva had his throne."

He then asked Amelia to describe Hindu worship. She laughed, as she noticed he was becoming more and more interested in her country, though the truth was that she was his prime motive and at that moment he wanted to kiss her, even though his sexual experience from youth had been nil.

"First," she began, "they bathe in the Ganges and put holy water in a brass vessel. They must also have some offerings – preferably money, say the Brahmins, guardians of our city. They go to the temple and bow towards its idol, walk round two or three times muttering prayers in the Sanskrit tongue asking for children and their hearts' desires, plus the destruction of enemies. Finally, they pour holy water on their idol and make their offering, after which the priest strikes the bell and poojah (worship) is over.

"They never ask for forgiveness or grace, and the priests boast to Leupolt that their god is greater than your Christian god because of its thousands of worshippers. His answer - that that the Christian god is the true god because the Hindu priests are always begging – seems wrong."

William laughed and said,

"He thinks their worship is just idolatory and sinfulness because you have more idols than people."

"He is almost certainly right on this."

William glanced towards the jungle outside the city, inhabited by Thugs and highway robbers, so that no one dare go out at night for fear of robbery and death. In this very place the central Church Missionary Society now stood.

"Leupolt thinks Hinduism and Islam are heathen: which do you prefer, Amelia, the Hindus or Muslims?"

Amelia paused and replied, "that's a big question. I am told my family were Hindu and there are bad things about Islam, as Leupolt will tell you, though it shares its Holy Book with the Christian story, which makes them competitors.

"Leupolt says much of the Koran is "mingled with error"; that their two versions of god are so different, Muslims cannot really have knowledge of the true god. In particular, Muslims think that because the Christian god is the author of both good and evil, He cannot therefore be a just god."

"You mean he is responsible for both good and bad?"

"Yes, and Christians think the Muslim paradise allows licentiousness. Not to mention, of course, they do not see Jesus as the Christ and put him below Mohammed, which is bound to annoy them."

William now asked Amelia about the Hindus:

"They are more complex and there is, says Leupolt, more hope for them. However, their holy books, the Vedas, show no knowledge of a 'true' god, for their god is 'the great nothing'."

William could not help laughing at the unusual juxtaposition of god and nothing. He needed to understand more about the 'nothing'.

"The problem for Leupolt is that the philosophers of Benares worship idols which represent the god of Brahm in many absurd forms, like ice and steam. To them, spirit and matter are the same, along with light and dark.

"To the Hindus, there is no real existence but Brahm and everything else is appearance. Creation is an illusion or *Maya*. We are a dream – nothing. As you Shakespeare says in his play, 'we are such stuff as dreams are made on, and our little life is rounded with a sleep.' "

Again, William could not help sniggering at this idea: "so what, then, is reality and how do you know it to distinguish sin from wickedness, like the Christians?"

He became even more puzzling when she replied, "The Hindus cannot distinguish between themselves and god, for they are one. We are all like little drops of water – part of, and the same as the great Ganges and we mix with the oceans.

"Leupolt thinks this is evil because If we are god, how can we also be holy like him and at the same time not sinful? If I lie, is it god, rather than me? Hindus say it is god and in this way they throw off responsibility for their own actions. Leupolt also says that their idol worship leads away from our god because their actions are corrupt.

"He thinks they worship the sun, moon, stars, rivers and many beasts – everything except the true god. They therefore worship devils, not god. Leupolt says their wisdom is foolishness and a nation is not superior to the gods it worships: that the Muslims are profligate and Hindus disregard truth. They are all slaves to Satan: what do you think?"

"What, about the caste system?" asked William. "In England we have a class system, but your caste system beats all because you cannot escape your caste. You have untouchables and priests, warriors, merchants and labouring classes that have no contact."

"If you ask me," replied Amelia, "every religion has its weaknesses because they are based on their own holy book with little basis in truth and littered with contradictions. Not to mention that it soon becomes out of date – that is, if it was ever historically accurate in the first place. There is no way to prove or disprove them, except by reason, which is entirely lacking in religion."

William thought the Hindus a contented people, who never thought about tomorrow and, more to the political point, would never rise against England: "They are easier than Muslims to control, because Muslims are united by Mohammed's commandment to kill unbelievers. Mark me, the day will come when we British will have to account for our treatment of our colonial Muslims – if not now, maybe soon."

"All Indians," replied Amelia, a little peeved that William was disregarding what the British were doing to all Indians, "have shown that they might rise and destroy all the British here, so you must be very careful how you rule, whatever, religion."

"But," interrupted William vehemently, "I do not like the idea of suttee – burning wives on the funeral pyres of their husbands. Women are not treated well here - perhaps even worse than in England."

"Things have improved a little," said Amelia, but they are still very bad. Leupolt does not think Hindus are a naturally cruel people, but their religion makes them so. And he says that the commandment 'love they neighbour as thyself' is unknown to both Muslims and Hindus."

William considered the way workers were treated in his own country and thought that selfish capitalism also had something to do with cruelty, as Karl Marx had argued. Then, returning to the discussion, he continued,

"But your caste system is definitely worse than our English classes, because you cannot climb out and better yourself to become 'clean'. It discourages self-improvement - in England we believe every person is an individual and can escape sin through right thinking, though it is not as easy as it sounds with selfish capitalists around. Hindus think they can only earn salvation by disgusting acts of self-deprivation, like hanging upside down for weeks, which has nothing to do with helping your fellow men. This is why Leupolt has built several chapels in Benares."

"So, what do **you** think of your England in India, William – a good or bad thing? What are your facts, Mr. Gradgrind?"

At the grand age of nearly twenty-three, William smiled and tried to summon up adequate wisdom so as not to offend Amelia's love of country, or his love of her:

"It taught us one thing, to be sure: never to have an army of less than fifty percent of the Indian force in arms and also not to train natives in artillery."

Amelia smiled at this military realism, "So you accept we Indians should not trust the British."

"Our queen Victoria has said we will not impose Christianity on India – "

"I wonder what Leupolt thinks about that – he's in India to convert us inferior 'heathen'! William, you will never rid us of our 'primitive' traditions, despite your arrogant Christianity."

"But," said William, "Victoria is now queen of all India and your Indian landowners are pleased to belong to her honours hierarchy."

"Mark my words, William, it won't be long before ordinary Indians begin to demand independence, like your Ireland and other colonies – and we will be watching very closely for your military weaknesses, as in Afghanistan and the Crimea. And I have no doubt that soon, African Zulus will rise up and make their mark against your arrogant little army. This country is only run for the benefit of you English. Our own industries are neglected and merely a source of raw materials, like cotton, to supply British industry in your mills. One day, we, too, will industrialize and threaten your Yorkshire and Lancashire cotton trade, showing how much you have used us. You will be sorry."

William thought immediately of his sisters back in their Pleasley mill and shuddered.

THE LACEY FAMILY, JANUARY 1914

Probably taken on the Lacey's golden wedding anniversary in January 1914. The writer's grandmother, Rose, is at the back in the middle, holding her first-born, Horace, brother of my father Thomas Samuel Merry. He would later become a bus driver and fight in Palestine during the Second World War. The writer's father would become a Bevan Boy in his Shirebrook coal mine.

William and Amelia

The writer's grandmother, Rose, with Amelia

MARRIAGE, JANUARY 7th, 1864

William and Amelia became ever more attracted to one another as they enjoyed talking about and exploring differences between England and India. so that he found as much time as possible to visit the mission. It was now the "cold" season, lasting from November to February, giving relief from the preceding Hot and Rainy season and they sealed their preordained love on a Christmas walk along the banks of the Ganges by the ghats, [9] preferable to the city's narrow streets.

The weather was delightful and renovating as they walked past the huge Arungzebe mosque, built by said emperor two hundred years before by destroying a Hindoo temple. On their walk a snake suddenly appeared and William, ever the gentleman, prepared to stamp on it, but a Hindu woman shouted at him, "Do not kill one of our gods!"

Amelia now told him more of her past life: her mother and father's death and her assignment to Leupolt's Orphan girl's school. She explained how, though the Orphan School was Christian in this city where Shiva was said to have reigned, her beliefs were not yet fixed and, though Leupolt was very insistent, she was still open-minded as to becoming a Christian.

---

[9] Steps leading down to the Ganges

"500,000 people live in Benares – one fifth Mohammedan, the rest Hindoos and 30,000 Brahmins. It is our holy city – the Athens of India, which attracts young men."

She then she sighed and said how beautiful was her world, making William think by contrast of his own home in Pleasley and how she might like it, for though it was different, he hoped one day to take her to England.

He suddenly took hold of her hand, which he had never done before, turning her towards him,

"Amelia, I think I am in love with you."

She had half expected this, for they had been building up to it since their first meeting at Leupolt's Mission's Sunday service. She was unexpectedly thrilled by his touch, promising a wonderful future, perhaps a big family and – possibly - a life in England.

"Or rather," added William, "I should say, I **know** I am in love with you. Will you marry me? I shall die if you say no." He was now absolutely sure in his hyperbole.

She smiled and affectionately hugged him for the first time, sure it that would last a lifetime. Though the present was settled, the future not yet: they needed to find somewhere to live and decide on a future family.

They passed several temples in the city where Shiva had had his throne, including Doorga, his wife, but Amelia was now William's "Shiva" and he devoted himself to discovering what she liked and wanted in their future life. They fixed their marriage with Leupolt for January 8th, 1864, to be attended by some of William's army colleagues – most famously, Lord Roberts, of future World War One fame – and a few of Amelia's Mission friends.

Amelia had told him there were far more idols in Benares than there were men. And she was pleased to know that the mission had been built on the spot where Thugs and highway robbers had operated because it meant that improvement was always possible.

William wanted to know more about Hinduism, despite Leupolt promise of as many converts to Christianity as Muslims. Amelia explained the Hindu worship of many gods – sun, moon, stars, trees, rivers, beasts - all of whom characters he had called "vile"

He had cruelly despised their wisdom as "foolishness"; their power as "weakness"; their love as hatred; their mercy cruelty; their holiness sin; and their chastity as licentiousness – all true pictures of sin

William and Amelia were married by Leupolt at the Church Missionary Society in Varanisi, where Amelia had lately been so happy. Leupolt had tutored her in the superiority of Christianity by telling her of the cruelties of the Hindu caste system and its treatment of women. He had said the commandment, "Thou shalt love they neighbour as thyself" was unknown to both Hindus and Mohammedans:

"The Muslims," he told her, "are enjoined by their religion to make war on their fellow-men if they differed in creed, while many a poor Hindu, taken ill on the road, is allowed to perish because no one can determine his caste, in order to decide whether they were allowed to help.

"When a servant delivering a message to my house left and was seized with cholera, he lay in the road from nine in the morning till three in afternoon and no one leant him a friendly hand. I hastened to his relief, but too late - he died. When I told the Indians, they said, "who can tell what caste the man is?" They feared that they might become unclean and lose their caste if they attended him."

Leupolt also liked to mention a class with no purpose but to commit murder: the Thugs, who worshipped the goddess of death, Kali, and felt no compunction in their crimes, simply because they were born Thugs.

William had read much about the thugs in Philip Meadows' 1839 book, *Confessions of a Thug* and it was said they had strangled thousands with their feared *roomal*, or scarf, robbing many Indians and even outwitted Robert Clive and the East India Company.

But Amelia told him that their influence was exaggerated by the British army to portray the English as bringing order to lawless India and not to take too much notice of its propaganda. She said it was a myth to justify British taking control of Mughal land.

In this sacred city of Benares, Ganges water was sacred and a mere drop could cleanse sins. Amelia asked William if he knew any nation more foolish than the English, who have shown it with their steam engines, paper mills and balloons? And similarly,

"When Leupolt told them the chronology of the Bible was true and unshaken and they were unable to stand before plain, simple, Gospel truths, they attacked him, first on the Trinity, which Christians called a revealed mystery and then on the authority of our scripture. They tried, said Leupolt, to to pick holes in our logic: 'you say that all men descended from Adam are sinners, which makes us all sinners. Then you tell us Christ was descended from Adam but was NOT a sinner. And you call this logic?'

"Leupolt told them Jesus was certainly without sin, even though he took on the body of an ordinary human, which they cannot accept. 'If God became man in Jesus, he could not have given up his essential holiness'. Then they insult me for the terrible conduct of the Europeans in India. The Indians laugh and mock me, blaspheming on the spot until I am obliged sometimes to leave my place of preaching.

"The Hindoos tell me my preaching is humiliating and they hate the name of Christ. They have received a prophecy that one day a nation will come from a foreign country and conquer them with the sword, after which they would start trying to diffuse their own religion here.

"You have," they said, "already conquered our bodies and now you try to conquer our minds."

Amelia was finally persuaded by Leupolt that her Hindu religion was wrong and sinful – but largely because of her youth and needful dependency on the mission for food and shelter. She could not argue with him – indeed she was barely old enough to have imbibed what Leupolt called the erroneous notions of her native religion, let alone worship the idols they say represent "God".

Now, the main thing was her love for William and their forthcoming marriage. She decided to take Leupolt's advice and wear white, rather than a colourful Indian costume, for he seemed struck on the Christian idea of purity. Besides, her love, was a Christian who knew nothing of Islam nor Hinduism. And like Leupolth, he had the English superiority over other religions. Nevertheless, she was very happy to have found a man she loved and looked forward to a marriage in tune with her husband's religion.

She was only fifteen and William twenty-seven – not uncommon in either India or England – and they both had romantic ideas about the ceremony, to which Leupolt added the idea of Christian purity, hence her pure white dress, which shone beside William's 2nd Dragoon redcoat, much admired by Lord Roberts, William's best man, hero of the Mutiny and future hero of World War One, in whose office he now worked at the local fort since leaving the regiment full time. Amelia was given away by a good friend in the Mission, who had been similarly educated in English. Otherwise, it was a quiet, momentous ceremony that would change her life.

After the marriage, they lived at William's fort Chunar, forty-five kilometres outside the city, where they had their first two children. Christopher was born in 1865 and was baptised at the 'church mission station' where William and Amelia married. However, Mary Margaret, would be born at Chunar, where they moved in 1869. It was quite clear they Amelia wanted a large family (fifteen), and she was happy to be consumed by childcare, which she saw as her life's mission after her own orphan life.

Although very happy, William wanted to take his wife to England, for which he began to make plans after he was invalided out of the army in 1870.

They left two children with friends, for fear they might be adversely affected by the long trip. They would later join the Laceys in England, but for the time being, would grow up in Varanasi under the care of Leupolt's mission, where they would be well-looked after by the church. Their parents had decided first to find a job and make a life for themselves in England before uniting the rest of the family.

William was excited to be going back home after thirteen years in India - his father had sadly died in 1862, so he was keen to introduce Amelia to mother, who was now seventy.

William and Amelia continued often to debate the Indian Mutiny and English double standards that could treat the Indians as savages, while at the same time treating them with murderous contempt in stealing their country. William became influenced by Amelia's version of events, while still retaining his British superiority, though he began to understand the titillating, false British accounts of how the Sepoys had sexually assaulted British women were false; and that Nana Sahib had a reason for disliking the British, though not for the disgusting Cawnpore killings of women and children. He began to appreciate that the British revenges had been re-doubled cruelty and terror, and not something to be proud of from a national pretending to be civilized.

He later recounted his adventures to mother, saying "I am proud that I have served my country, as every true British man should do...my regiment left me at Cawnpore with the remount horses (I was only 22 and Father was a groom). When they took my horse away from me and I threatened I would follow and get into the firing line, for it was dull enough work looking after horses when I just wanted to have a smack at the mutineers."

BACK TO ENGLAND (1870)

William received an order by telegraph to return to England on 19th January, 1870. His regiment had been given the option of remaining in India by transferring to other regiments, or sailing home. Fifty-eight men stayed behind and the rest marched from Sailkot on 23rd Jan for Lahore on 27th where they handed over arms, saddlery and horses and took train to Bombay, embarking on 28th Feb. But their ship, the *Euphrates,* unfortunately collided with another vessel in the harbour, delaying their departure until 5th March.

Unlike 2018, England did not then require a passport for Amelia's entry. Since 1815, the British had been hosts to many: Jews fleeing from pogroms, immigrants from continental autocracies like Russia, the Habsburg Empire and Italy, and, of course, Karl Marx.

In 1854, Ferdinand de Lesseps, former French consul to Cairo, had secured an agreement with the Ottoman governor of Egypt to build a canal 100 miles across the Isthmus of Suez, thus reducing the journey to England by weeks. An international team of engineers drew up a construction plan, and in 1856 the Suez Canal Company was formed, given the right to operate the canal for 99 years after completion of the work.

It was completed in 1869, so William and the *Euphrates* reached Suez on 18th March, where he re-embarked on the 'Crocodile' at Alexandria on 31st, bound for Portsmouth and arriving on 8th April. The voyage had taken just over a month compared with the three months spent on William's outward trip round Africa.

When it opened, the Suez Canal was only 25 feet deep, 72 feet wide at the bottom, and 200 to 300 feet wide at the surface. Consequently, fewer than 500 ships navigated it in its first full year of operation. William and Amelia were excited to be sailing one-hunded-and-one miles from the Mediterranean to the Red Sea on the "Canal des Deux Mers" (Canal of the Two Seas).

The canal's construction had required a vast workforce of Egyptian peasants, who were drafted in at a rate of 20,000 every ten months to carry out the work by hand with picks and shovels, though in 1863 Ismail Pasha who banned the use of forced labour. In response, the Suez Canal Company brought in steam and coal-powered shovels and dredgers that completed the removal of the seventy-five million cubic meters of sand required to create the canal.

When completed, Ismail treated his guests to a lavish stay and the partying continued for several weeks, taking boat trips on the Nile, eating in ancient temples or beneath tents in the desert decorated in red and yellow satin. There were traditional Arab ceremonies featuring music, dancers, Bedouin horsemen, and fire-eaters. And for the opening ceremony itself, special wooden seating areas were constructed covered with flowers, banners and other adornments for thousands of guests to witness the inauguration, followed by a dazzling fireworks display.

In 1875 Britain purchased Egypt's shares in the canal and seven years later, invaded and occupied the country following a nationalist uprising which it thought threatened the canal.

Five years after William and Amelia came back to England, Disraeli kept the French out of buying the Canal by insisting, against cabinet disapproval, that England buy it, assisted by four million pounds from the banker Rothschild ("it is just settled; you have it, Madam"). William wished he had enough money to purchase shares, for this was one of the best financial decisions made by a British government and would be a great assistance to British imperial dominance in India and China.

ENGLAND 1870

In 1870, William and Amelia landed at Portsmouth, naval centre of the great British Empire, where the *Victory*, headquarters of its fleet, floated proudly in the harbour. Amelia shivered when she arrived in England and took some time to adjust to its changeable temperatures.

Britain's leading politicians, Disraeli and Gladstone, were fighting over how to extend the vote after the 1819 Peterloo massacres without further frightening the landowners, how to deal with poverty and control the biggest empire the world had ever seen.

William had earned the much-coveted Indian Mutiny Medal and his discharge Papers recorded: "his conduct has been good and he is in possession of four good conduct badges", but he had been invalided out and must find a new job.

After a brief stay in London, showing Amelia the famous sights, including the new Houses of Parliament, Trafalgar Square and Victoria's Buckingham Palace, they returned to Mansfield's Pleasley Vale to introduce Amelia to his mother (minus father now deceased), brothers and sisters.

Amelia quickly took to her new family like Indian tea, and William noticed one big change around Pleasley – the new coal pits: "the collieries made a wonderful lot of difference, for when I first knew Mansfield, it was a small town, an agricultural centre. When, one by one, the collieries were opened the whole aspect of the town seemed to change and it forged ahead and increased in prosperity... (as a) rapidly increasing metropolis of a huge coal mining district." In the twentieth century, the author's family, including father, would work in the mines.

William was to live the rest of his life – some forty years - in Mansfield and for the first eighteen years after returning from India was employed at Mr Pye's wood turning and bobbin mills in Victorian St., before taking up insurance work, where he was to meet a fellow-agent who would marry William's daughter Rose, mother of the writer's father.

Finally, William and Amelia moved to 66 Stockwell Gate with his large family, where he lived for his last twenty-five years. From 1900, he was confined to house through illness and with four sons and eleven daughters, his fiftieth wedding anniversary in January 1914 was attended by twenty-four of his family, with the only other Mutiny veteran in Mansfield.

Prime Minister, Benjamin Disraeli's 1867 Reform Act had tried to mend some of the differences between what he called the "Two Nations", so vividly demonstrated by the Peterloo Massacre of 1819. Five out of six adult males still did not vote and no woman could.

William's opinion on the great political debate then taking place was that it was a necessary development so long denied English working people, though he was old fashioned enough to believe that women did not need it because their men looked after them. In fact, Disraeli's act brought household suffrage with simple occupancy, rather than the previous 1832 £10 requirement in rates - a new electorate of 44%, but still no women! William was at last enfranchised and nostalgically recalled old discussions with his dead father about the infamous 1819 Peterloo Massacre, one of whose aims was "no taxation without representation". He would live just long enough to see the enfranchisement of women and total democracy for men in 1918.

The big question had been whether everyone would get the vote, regardless of wealth? Certainly not, thought the governments of the day: but Peterloo and the 1832 Reform Act had begun the process of British democracy, though it was by no means accepted.

To which side did she and William belong? His father had taught him to hope and fight for democracy against the grasping mill owners and aristocracy.

But there were still great political divisions in Britain between reformers and the old ruling aristocracy over democracy and the extension of the vote, despite false national myths about England as a centre of decency, tolerance and a sense of fair play. In fact, England was choc-a-bloc with class hatred - the aristocracy insisting that the working class were only a breath away from a French revolutionary mob and therefore resorting, as so often since, to institutional brutality.

Carlisle, for example, criticized the new industrial Britain as "pot-bellied, sunk in its own dirty fat and offal and of a stupidity defying the gods." He thought the vote for ordinary people "vulgar, absurd and block-headed". There were, in fact, great political divisions in Britain between reformers and the old ruling aristocracy over democracy and the extension of the vote.

And Amelia was in a country where she experienced firsthand the racism she had already seen in India. William was one of the rare army exceptions who had taken an Indian wife, though discouraged from doing so after the Mutiny. In Mansfield Amelia expected racist comments and wondered how William would feel about protecting her reputation while at the same time, defending his own and England's colonial record.

He did not like talk of Amelia's supposed racial inferiority and whether her children would be worth less than whites. This did not stop them having fifteen children in all – perhaps to win the Evolutionary argument by superiority in numbers.

Apart from India's enormous empire – "the jewel in the crown" - England's colonies now included Canada, S. Africa, Australia and New Zealand, the W. Indies, and W. Africa. And its possessions continued to grow, so that there was never a year in which the English were not fighting at some point in the world.

Perhaps William saw Amelia simply as a colonial prize after his Indian war, though he was a kind man who never treated her badly. As for her children, they were sensitive about being "half-castes" and did not like to speak about it, which may have been the reason that the present writer was never told about his family history.

While caring for her many children, Amelia quickly noticed that England's superior attitude towards the people of the British Empire – especially the blacks - was coarsening and remembered that the Indians had always been referred to as "niggers" during the Mutiny. Some still respected the Indians and their culture, but they were decreasing: and Tennyson himself complained to Gladstone, "We are more tender to the blacks than to ourselves…niggers are tigers, niggers are tigers."

And Amelia soon learned that most English thought her race savage, lazy, criminal and apathetic, only good for subjugation. Britain was already involved in the conquest of Africa, causing the military disaster in 1879 at the hands of the Zulus at Isandlwana. So much, she thought, for Uncle Tom and freeing the slaves!

Way after the Mutiny, she noticed the English continued to despise Indians, so that even though they were to provide 1.5 million men in the future

World War One, with 34,000 deaths, they would be forgotten, ignored, treated with brutality and prejudice, and white-washed from History.

In 1876, Queen Victoria - the new "Empress of India", completed for Amelia the total subjugation of her lovely country when she visited it. Though William was proud, she was disgusted at Disraeli's unbounded "cheek" in treating her country as a mere appendage and could not forget that England was the richest nation in the world only because of its possession of colonies like her India.

Victoria ruled only because of Britain's naval firepower and the argument that free trade spread peace did not appeal to her at all. The British navy and army alone were the cause of its influence, which is why she saw its wars being fought every year in some part of the world. In fact, free trade meant blood spilled all over the world and not one year without war. Despite Cardwell's army reforms, most soldiers still usually joined the army out of poverty and ignorance – like the Irish and her mill-worker husband, William.

And even in this rich colonial English nation, life was nasty, brutish, short and dirty, with no childhood for the poor, working in factories from an early age, marrying young and raising weakly children in filthy, overcrowded hovels. Disraeli was right, England was a land of two nations and she would not live to see democracy.

She had already seen Christianity as a spearhead for British colonialism in the Varanasi Missionary society, though happy to be a Christian close to William, and learning the English which had made possible her marriage in the first place; but though one of her daughters would marry into William Booth's Salvation Army which had done did so much to help the poor, she only reluctantly accepted her national duality, suppressing love of her native country which she loved dearly because she loved William.

The new European politics were difficult to adjust to: France's Napoleon III would soon declare war on Prussia, and suffer a bloody defeat, laying the first foundations of German "greatness" and the future horrible First World War. Queen Victoria's daughter had married the ruler of Prussia, and Germany was united by Bismarck only after war, in the Versailles Hall of Mirrors, a grand humiliation for the French.

William was not sure whether he supported the French or Germans, though he retained a historic dose of English hatred of Napoleon 1st, as well as bitter memories of French superiority in the Crimean - he therefore rather sympathised with Queen Victoria's daughter and her husband in Germany, thus continuing the hatred that seemed to drive politics in Europe.

Amelia was impressed to learn that in 1870 there would be a new system of universal secular education for everyone under thirteen, but when she thankfully mentioned to William that this meant for the first time working classes learning to read and write, he strongly disagreed:

"Nonsense, most people can already read and write, so there is really no need for Forster's act. It is rather, more likely to be a government ploy of control. And, my dear, it is not free, unless you can prove you are poor."

Darwin's theories were also being discussed and when the pope declared his infallibility, which Amelia thought rather pompous superiority, she found Darwin's idea that her own body bore the stamp of an ape un-religiously refreshing because it also questioned English superiority by placing them on the same level.

William looked at his newspaper:

"This man, Darwin, says he has finally solved the mystery of mysteries – the origin of life on earth."

Amelia said, "God created the world and everything in it – why doesn't he read his Bible?"

"That's just it," said William, "he says in this book that we are all descended from one biological source of organism. He also explains why giraffes have got long necks."

"In his wisdom," replied Amelia, "surely God gave them long necks so they could reach their food in the trees and not starve to death."

"Ah, but Darwin says that giraffes **'grew'** long necks in order to be able to reach the food, so after creation, they couldn't originally reach it."

"How on earth did they do that? Once a giraffe, always a giraffe! They can't go on growing."

"Well, he says that some giraffes have longer necks because of an accident of nature and pass them on to their offspring through an accident of nature."

"Impossible! How on earth can you pass on accidents? Anyway, surely a giraffe is a giraffe and has not changed since God created it in the Garden of Eden."

"It does sound rather mad, doesn't it? Darwin's all about the struggle for survival in Nature. Short necks die out and long necks survive. It's all competition – the in-word of our modern capitalist world – he calls it 'selective breeding', as in horse-racing. Apparently he was influenced by Malthus theory of population and his book is now a best seller."

"So where does God come into all this? And who set off the whole train of creation in the first place, if it wasn't God."

"Well, he might still have created everything, but the problem is that things started changing, which means God is no longer necessary except as the *primum mobile*, or first mover and this annoys religious people –".

"Well, Christians, anyway," said Amelia

"Biology, Chemistry and accidents are the new god. He is no longer necessary. Life created itself, or evolved, in a long process. Darwin's wife, Emma, who is very religious, does not like his theory one bit and it is causing him much heart-searching – his scientific head versus her sentimental heart."

"Not surprising," replied Amelia. "The Church won't be very pleased by this atheist challenge to their authority. So, how were we created?"

"Listen to this," replied William, "it is very funny: in an Oxford debate the Bishop Wilberforce wanted to know whether it was through his grandfather or grandmother that he claimed descent from a monkey. Huxley replied that since the Bishop was being so ridiculous challenging science, he himself would rather have been descended from a monkey! Ha! Ha!"

"But this is serious: Fitzroy, captain of the *Beagle*, committed suicide over it in 1865. And I am frightened that the whole of our Christian beliefs are now being pooh poohed."

"Perhaps God is responsible for evolution – he created the first animals – including man – and left nature to get on with its own development, according to his laws. And apparently we are not descended from the monkeys, anyway, we are only their cousins, though descended from a common source."

"But if nature really is red in tooth and claw, and there is no purpose in life, where does out loving God fit into all this? And how can an animal that has never flown suddenly develop wings, or a sea creature suddenly start breathing air? It doesn't make sense."

"Darwin says that nature favours those accidents that help animals survive, and that includes us and, maybe, our brains – though I do not rate human intelligence, which will one day destroy our beautiful earth."

William picked up his family Bible, in which all the names of his family were written on the inside cover and pondered for a while:

"This Evolution thing seems a bit far-fetched, so I think I will go on reading and believing what is in this old scripture." He tapped the cover. "It makes more sense. I agree with Gladstone, who is opposed to the new Divorce Bill because divorce is a sin and marriage made in heaven."

"I think," said Amelia, "that God made us the way we were, that animals change due to competition for food and the best adapted survive. Perhaps God only started the world off –"

"True," said William, "but then natural selection does away with the idea of a creator, if things are changing all the time in response to the environment."

William laughed once more to read out Bishop of Wilberforce's comic question - whether it was through his grandfather or grandmother that he was descended from a monkey. Huxley's answer was just as funny – he said he would rather have had an ape than people who introduced ridicule into a grave scientific discussion.

Amelia thought that was funny, but worried that God might no longer be the creator and there was no purpose in life, apart from British capitalist competition.

"It is queer," she said, "to be asked to believe that we are all descended from one original life form... And how do all those giraffes know that they need a long neck, anyway?"

***

William and Amelia lived in Mansfield for forty years in total. For eighteen years, he was employed at Mr Pye's wood turning and bobbin mills in Victorian St., before taking up insurance work, when they moved into Mansfield's 66, Stockwell Gate to be closer to the people William was servicing for insurance.

However, from 1900, he was confined to home through illness from his war in India, while Amelia took on most the work of raising their numerous family.

January 1914 was their fiftieth wedding anniversary. With four sons and eleven daughters. Twenty-four in all attended, along with the only other Mutiny veteran in Mansfield.

The Great War was about to begin, but of course, they had little inkling of its causes, as yet, though they had been in the making since France's defeat in 1870. Amelia died of bronchitis in 1918 at the age of sixty-five and William, who was now confined permanently to his home because of bad health, returning to family to die in Mexborough, 1919 at the age of eighty- five.

POSTSCRIPT

As my distant relation mentions, this book changes one's view of oneself completely and it is interesting to learn that in a recent analysis of my political outlook I am seen as part of the *Global Green Community:*

Global Green Community clan members combine an array of socialist views on the economy, with liberal and environmentalist stances on social issues. Their version of socialism has distinctly environmentalist overtones. GGC members have a strongly civic interpretation of Britishness, little interest in the nation-state and want governments to pursue an ethical and inclusive foreign policy.

I have travelled the globe, beginning the age of twenty-seven with a motor-bike trip to Egypt and latterly living in China from 1999-2008.

Did my history have something to do with William's internationalism? My younger brother, who lives in Singapore and travels the world, also married Malaysian Muslim, though after thinking about it, he did not convert.

I like to think that William Lacey's adventurous spirit continued into future generations, though my brother and I are teachers not warriors.

SOME CORRESPONDENCE WITH A FELLOW DESCENDENT OF WILLIAM AND AMELIA

After advertising in Mansfield Museum and recording a Radio 4 interview about my great grandparents in 2010 (*Who Do You Think You Are?*), I was contacted by Richard, descendant of one of the older Lacey sons who interestingly looked more English than Indian.

He wrote:

Der Sam,

"my ancestor Mary eventually married a member of the East India Company on St Helena but not for a number of years, after two of their children had been born. I've found, in researching them, that although relations between slaves and members of the English East India Company on St Helena were theoretically forbidden, they actually happened relatively frequently, especially in the lower ranks of the EIC-controlled St Helena Regiment. It did make me realise that the social mores on St Helena were often surprisingly relaxed because of the physical distance between Britain and the island.

If you can possibly find the original pieces of the torn photo and send me scans I should be able to restore them digitally back together into one image. The finished result depends a little on how much of the original surface has been lost but it's a fairly straight-forward process.

I recently had an operation on my throat so email is probably the best means of communication for now. If I think of anything else, I'll let you know. I wish I had more concrete information to share.

Best wishes, Richard

Dear Richard.

Thanks for your information. I meant to ask your profession – are you retired? I hope you throat injury was not too serious. I talked to a local man from St Helena last week and asked about the new airport, which he says is because of the Falklands.

You raise some interesting points, which make more sense than the Begum story if, in fact, Amelia was an orphan. And, yes, your great-great uncle does not look Indian, does he? By the way, have you been to India? I only stopped briefly in New Delhi when my Chinese wife and I returned to our Chinese home a couple of years ago. And I also drew a blank making official enquires about marriage certificates.

Sam

Richard

Many thanks for your reply and photo. Excuse my tardiness in responding but I have been away for the weekend. No I am not yet retired. I was in France working with someone who constructed timber-framed houses but decided to return following the Brexit Vote. I am not thinking of going back as adjusting to the UK is difficult - for me anyway. We'll see.

I hope you find the Leupolt memoirs interesting. In many ways, his writing feels like the closest we'll ever get to William and Amelia themselves. He married them and, in a very tangible way, lived a similar existence in the same place. When he talks about the climate and the locals and the wildlife, they are things they must have experienced themselves.

I think I have got most of the items you listed in your email. The wedding anniversary and funeral reports are interesting although, disappointingly, Amelia's voice is almost totally absent. I would like to know more about her background and what life was like for her in India and as the mother of a strikingly multi-racial family living in Mansfield. Family history has certainly changed my views. I assumed, prior to starting it ten or twelve years ago, that I was largely English. It was a surprise to find not only a lot of recent Irish and Dutch ancestors, but also the Indian and non-European ancestry from St. Helena. It has certainly made me think differently about both myself and the nature of nationality.

I have not given up hope of finding more re: the Laceys in India. I have not visited India, but would very much like to. I am going to investigate the missionary archives at Birmingham University. I you ever get hold of the original of the ripped photo of William and Amelia, then please send me a scan

With best wishes,

Richard

OTHER BOOKS UNDER SAM MERRY ON *AMAZON*

Futures Past – autobiography

Dragon Chasing the Sun – essays from China, 2002-2008

What Did Christianity Ever Do for Me? – autobiographical analysis of the effects of religion on the author's life

The Construction of 20th Century History – how historians work with some 20th century themes

China Against the Tides – diary of China in 2014, the year of the Horse

A Faraway Country – a semi-autobiographical novel set in Prague

China love – Love across the world that Begins to turn Chinese

Real China Love – semi-autobiographical novel set in Guangdong, China

Travellers in an Antique Land – account of adventures in Cairo after travelling to teach there by motorbike, 1975-6

Eighties Blues - a woman's life in Mrs Thatcher's England. Nothing's changed!

Blue Cheese and Chao Mian – an Englishman brings his Chinese love to live in England, with comic effects

Silly History – Student comedy based on thirty years teaching History